White Girl

white girl

Sylvia Olsen

sononis PRESS
WINLAW, BRITISH COLUMBIA

LIBRARY AND ARCHIVES CANADA CATALOGUING IN PUBLICATION

Olsen, Sylvia, 1955-
White girl / Sylvia Olsen.

ISBN 1-55039-147-X

I. Title.
PS8579.L728W47 2004 jC813'.6 C2004-905974-2

Sono Nis Press most gratefully acknowledges the support for our publishing program provided by the Government of Canada through the Book Publishing Industry Development Program (BPIDP), the Canada Council for the Arts, and the British Columbia Arts Council.

First printing: November 2004
Second printing: September 2005

Edited by Laura Peetoom

Published by
Sono Nis Press
Box 160
Winlaw, BC V0G 2J0
1-800-370-5228

Distributed in the U.S. by
Orca Book Publishers
Box 468
Custer, WA 98240-0468
1-800-210-5277

books@sononis.com
www.sononis.com

Printed and bound in Canada by Kromar

To my children Joaquim, Adam, Joni, and
Heather, and grandchildren Yetsa and Maddison
who have taught me so much about colour.

I started school at Regent's Institute for the Arts in September, three months ago. The other day a guy was making small talk with me in the cafeteria, and he asked me where I was from. The question stumped me. I thought of saying the city where I grew up and now feel like a tourist. Then I thought of saying I come from the Indian reserve where I've lived for the past three years. It's home, it's where my family is – but it's not really where I'm from. So I told him a long-winded story about being raised in the city and then moving to the Indian reserve when I was fifteen. And now, I said, I don't really know where I'm from. The guy said, Really, with a strange look on his face and continued to munch on his sandwich. That was the end of our conversation.

So I'm sitting here in my dorm room, listening to CDs, rubbing the smooth green stone Grandma gave me between my fingers, and staring at a blank piece of paper. I'm trying to think of 500 words to write for my communications class about why I like to draw. It's a simple question, but once again I'm stumped. My mind keeps flitting back to the guy in the cafeteria and the look on his face when I gave him my stupid convoluted answer. I think the two questions are tied together, although I'm not exactly sure how. I like to draw because I like to look at things, study things, present things from different perspectives.

And the reason I like to look at things from different perspectives probably has to do with where I'm from. Or at least where I've been. It's going to take a lot more than 500 words, but if I get it straight about where I'm from, then it'll be easy to write 500 words about perspective and why I like to draw.

It happened when I was fifteen. That was the year my life was turned upside down, inside out, and back to front. Talk about perspective.

If you knew me when I was fifteen, you wouldn't have given me a moment's notice. We, Mom and me, lived in town. Not a big city, but not that small either. Big enough to have five theatres and three decent-sized shopping malls. There were at least a dozen apartments taller than fifteen floors – like ours – and five or six high schools in the area.

Josie Jessop. Josephine Joanne Jessop to be exact. I was five feet three-and-a-quarter inches tall if I stretched and held my heels slightly off the floor. Ninety-six pounds, with my clothes on. Blonde hair – for-real, naturally golden blonde, the kind everybody tries to match. My eyes were baby blue most of the time. When I stared into the mirror they reflected light like pools of water – dark sometimes, light sometimes, grey, turquoise, even kind of green when I wore certain colours.

My skin? It was pale, no doubt about it. I had a few milky freckles that were only visible when it was really hot, and I tanned dark in the summer – at least dark for someone so blonde. And that's about it. Nothing special. Not someone people turn around and look at twice. Not someone who people point at and say, "Look at her." Sort of boring really. So I never gave myself that much thought – I mean about my skin or my colour. If someone had asked me to describe my skin, I suppose I would have said white. But then, who would have asked?

I remember thinking about it once when a girl and I were looking at a poster that was hanging in my grade eight social studies room, advertising an international conference. It had a large circle in the centre, divided into four parts. Each quarter was a different colour – yellow, red, black, and white. There were pictures of people in each colour, and sprawled across the bottom were the words *Many Colours, One World*. Goofy, but not something I had thought of before. The girl said her dad came from the Philippines, so that made her a yellow person. For a fleeting second I thought, I must be a white person. The truth is, I thought I was transparent – no colour at all.

In our city there were people from other places, sure. Chinese people lived up the road; the kids went to private school. Black people from Jamaica worked at the dry cleaner and florist. Pakistanis or East Indians or whatever you call them lived a few blocks away – it seemed like hundreds of them lived in a row of old houses painted bright colours like purple and orange and gold. And tons of Japanese tourists bused to town in the summer. But other than that I lived in a white city, no doubt about it. And white people were just people. They were the people that stood in the centre and looked out. They were the background colour, the ambient noise, they blended in. It was the other people who stuck out.

I wouldn't have described it like that before I moved. It's only by looking back that I can say I even noticed being white. Until I was fifteen, I was just a girl. Mom would have told you that I was self-centred and thought I was too good to be true. She would have called me a handful (she loved calling me a handful), with a mind of my own and grown up before my time. That was because it was just her and me, and half the time she was busy acting like a kid so somebody had to be grown up. I might have been a handful, but I was still a good girl, at least in Mom's eyes. I mean, I didn't do any obviously bad stuff she could find out about. Like if I was going to drink or smoke up or anything, I made sure she didn't know – it was easier that way. I was normal, whatever that means. I hung out with an okay crowd – my friends Sarah and Katy were cool. I was a good-enough student – Bs mostly (without trying).

You know how they say that you can't really see what one thing is until it is set beside something else? For instance, a guy looks really tall when he is standing beside a short guy. But if he was in a room with all tall guys, you wouldn't even notice. Or like someone looks pretty rich when they hang around poor people, but you wouldn't even notice they were rich if they were with a bunch of other rich people. Everything is relational – one thing next to the other. That's how we figure things out. That's how it was when we lived in the city, where almost everyone was like me – I blended in.

Then with one move I became a white girl, painted like a picket fence – plain as day, whiter than white. I became the kind of thing that would catch people's eyes if they were walking down the street – look how white that thing is. As if the sun was reflecting off me like a brand-new nickel – blinding – no getting around it, no hiding it, no missing what colour I was. I was in the spotlight. I hated it. I would have done anything to escape – if I had more guts, which is another story. I couldn't stand the heat and wanted to run back to somewhere that I could melt into the crowd and be anonymous again.

It began simply enough: Mom met Martin. They fell in love. Like a bolt of lightning out of nowhere (that's how Mom put it).

It was early Sunday morning. I had snuck in around 2 a.m., expecting Mom to be asleep in her room. She wasn't. That should have been my first clue that something strange was happening. Mom only went out about once in a thousand years, and when she did she was always home by midnight. I thought about heading back out, but then I decided when Mom got home she would probably check to see if I was in bed. So I curled up on the sofa and watched *Three's Company* reruns on TV until I fell asleep. It was 3:30 or 4 a.m. when Mom finally barged in the door. Her eyes were bugged wide open and her makeup was smudged around her cheeks and lips as if she'd been rubbing up against something. When she plunked herself next to me, she had a smile on her face as big as a kid at a birthday party. She looked forty going on fifteen. She threw her arms around me and planted a sloppy wet kiss on my cheek.

I was shocked. Mom wasn't the sort of person to be giddy, and she'd never been one to kiss me right out of the blue. She only kissed me on my birthday or Christmas or on my forehead to check for a fever. Mom had what you could call a permanent case of semi-depression. She walked through life as if she was constantly negotiating a space for herself between low cloud cover and quicksand. Life for Mom was a series of scary possibilities to be avoided at all costs. Her mantra was "Yeah, but." If I said, "It's a great day," she would say, "Yeah, but the weatherman says it's going to rain." If I said, "I got a B in socials, pretty good, eh?" she would say,

"Yeah, but you could have got an A if you handed your assignment in on time." If I asked her if she had a good sleep she would say, "Yeah, but I know I won't sleep good tonight. I can never get two good nights' sleep in a row."

So when she flew in the door that night, looking like she had had the time of her life, I was caught by surprise.

"I'm in love," she blurted out. That was it. *I'm in love,* followed by no *but* – no qualifier.

"Like a bolt of lightning out of nowhere," she said. "I didn't see it coming, but it came right across the dance floor and swept me off my feet and waltzed me away."

That was just the beginning. Mom talked until the birds started chirping. She talked more to me that night than she had talked to me in my whole life before that moment or since. She and Gina had been out at the OK Corral, a country-and-western dance bar. Mom described in minute detail every dance, every look, every touch, what her friends said, what she said, who was at the nightclub, the music. You name it, I heard about it. And most of all, she talked about Martin Angus, who was the real point of all her enthusiasm.

"He's a real ponytail Indian," gushed Mom. "Nothing like other Indians. He wore the most awesome cream-coloured cowboy boots and GWG jeans. God, Jo Jo, you should see how his jeans fit. Snug, like this, over his butt." She leaned over and motioned with her hands, two perky cheeks.

"And his leather jacket." She closed her eyes and pulled in a long breath as if she could still smell his cologne. "Oh, Jo Jo, he is a sexy man." She thought for a moment, dreamy like, still with her eyes closed. "He's a combination between Harvey Keitel and Antonio Banderas."

Can you imagine? I thought of some exotic guy who

looked like he had been run over by a train. Apparently he was the best line dancer in the club, and he could waltz.

"Holy cow. You should have seen him waltz," she said. "No, you should have *felt* him waltz."

"No, Mom," I said. "I shouldn't have."

I was half disgusted (you should have seen her; she had the hots for him like crazy) and half excited for her. That night Martin waltzed Mom right out of her depression (at least for a while). She was happy and I couldn't help but be happy as well, although I had no idea what would follow.

That was March or April. Within two weeks, Mom and I were driving out to the Indian reserve so she could stay with Martin on the weekends. That's what Martin called the place. And according to Martin, that's what he was – an Indian. Not Aboriginal, First Nations, indigenous, native, or any other makeshift PC name, he said. He said all the stuff – good and bad – that people thought when they heard the word "Indian" had to do with him, and changing the name wasn't going to take that away.

I didn't know there was such a thing as an Indian reserve, never mind one less than an hour away from town. I also didn't know the difference between First Nations, Indians, Aboriginals, natives, or whatever you were supposed to call them. I had heard about First Nations in school – a few chapters in our Canadian history textbook – explorers, wars, pemmican (that dried meat stuff that sounded revolting), buffalo, and beaver pelts. Mavis (Mom's mom, who refused to be called Grandma or Nana) said some (not very good) stuff about Indians in Winnipeg, where she lived, but I never paid any attention. Once in a while, if there was a protest on the news or a TV program about treaties or something, I overheard Mom and her friends complaining that Indians wanted to take over all the land and not pay any taxes. Gina would roll her eyes and smack her lips and say Indians drank too much. Then they would change the channel. And there were the Indians I saw downtown. Weird, I thought. Why did so many Indians live on the streets? But I never thought of the answers. What did I care?

I was okay with going to Martin's place for the first couple of weekends. I didn't believe Mom and Martin really had anything serious going on. I thought Mom was kicking her heels up, and I'd never seen her do that before, so I wanted to share it with her. Mom and Martin disappeared and I slept a lot, curled up on the sofa, caught up on homework, and ignored everyone. I thought Mom would get over it. Then, after a few weeks, I got tired of spending weekends out in the middle of nowhere. I missed my friends. Especially Sarah and Katy. I missed the parties, guys, opportunities, and everything.

One Sunday evening just before summer holidays, after a weekend on the reserve, Mom and I pulled into the car park at the apartment. It felt good to be home. Everything looked great – the dingy basement lights covered with cobwebs and dead flies, the bulging parched wooden fence ready to fall down any moment, and the laundry steam belching out of the vent into our parking space. During the drive home, I had made up my mind. That was the last time I was going out to the reserve with Mom. I had worked out in my head what I would say. I'd tell her that she could have her love affair and I would stay home, stay at Sarah's or Katy's, wherever, but I wasn't going out with her to Martin's place again. Before I had time to speak, even before she turned off the car, Mom blurted out, "Martin and I are meant to be together. Forever."

She caught me right out of the blue.

"We're getting married," Mom said, as calmly as if she had said, We're going out for dinner.

I didn't believe her. Ever since Dad left she'd been saying, "Marriage is something, honey, you only do once. After that you figure out that all that stuff about forever after is for people like Cinderella. And honey, there ain't no such thing as Cinderella."

Then Mom said, "After the wedding, we're moving into Martin's house."

After the frigging *what?* I thought maybe if I laughed it would turn out to be a joke. But her eyes met mine directly. She lifted her chin and gave me a look that said, No fooling, I know exactly what I'm doing. It wasn't a look I was used to, not with Mom.

"What do you mean?" I gasped.

Mom, up to that moment, had been totally predictable. I could count on knowing where she was and what she would be doing – which wasn't very much. I knew what she was going to say before she said it. Before that moment, Mom's life, if you could call it a life, consisted of watching TV and visiting a few girlfriends who lived in the apartment. Every few months they went out to a club or for drinks, and I could count on Mom coming home bored and crabby.

"We're going to be a family," said Mom, and she might as well have added, "and we're going to live happily ever after." So much for there being no such thing as Cinderella.

I decided Mom had gone nuts. Seriously nuts. Go to live in the boonies – are you crazy? On an Indian reserve? Mom, are you out of your mind? I was a city girl, blacktop and concrete, parking lots and the mall.

"That's it?" I shouted and instantly turned maniacal. "And

don't I get some say in where I live?"

I yanked my knapsack out of the back seat, slammed the car door, and raced up the road. "I'm never coming home," I shouted, but I doubt Mom heard me. "Never. I can take care of myself."

Which, of course, wasn't true. I stayed with Sarah for a few days. Her mom said it was okay, but I'd have to leave in a week or two. Then I stayed at Katy's for a while. Her mom wanted me to move in.

"*Indian* reserves are no place for a girl like you," she said when Katy asked if I could live at her house. "*Indians* are dangerous. They aren't like us. I can't believe your mom would do something like that."

She said the word "Indian" like it was background music to a horror movie. Later Katy's dad agreed with what her mom said about the reserve and Mom, but he said they had no room for another kid permanently, so I went back home in time for the wedding.

After a weekend honeymoon, Mom borrowed a pickup truck and hauled my bed, her bedside table, the television, our clothes, and a few other things over to Martin's place. I stayed out with Sarah and Katy until Mom came looking for me.

"Jo Jo," she said. Her eyes bobbed from me to the load on the truck and then back to the apartment. "Isn't this exciting? It's the first day of the rest of our lives."

Way to go, Mom, I thought. You must be the last of the original thinkers. I slumped in the seat and closed my eyes. I didn't sleep. I had a lump in my stomach and felt like I was going to puke until we arrived.

And there I was. Home on the reserve. The summer holiday from hell. Forty minutes from civilization. No buses and no car – Mom sold the old piece of crap we had.

"We don't need it," she had said when Gina gave her 200 bucks for it. "We can use Martin's car."

I was trapped, no way out. No friends. I talked to Sarah and Katy non-stop on the phone until it was disconnected, and then I bawled and bawled and bawled. Mom said Martin was going to hook the phone back up, but if I'd held my breath waiting for it, I would have turned blue and died – the phone didn't get reconnected for months. Mom also said things would be better and I'd get over it as soon as I started at the new school, something I dreaded and didn't want to think about.

I retreated to my room. I had that, at least. Martin said he didn't think that it was right for me to sleep on the sofa. So he hauled out stacks of stuff he had stored in the spare room – piles of magazines, broken furniture, bicycles, car parts, laundry baskets full of blankets, old clothes, and everything else that a house doesn't need but that the owner keeps if he has space. When the room was clean, Mom set up my bed and put on my own sheets and comforter. I wrapped myself in my sheets like a mummy and pulled my comforter over my head, then fell into sleep like I was being rocketed into a dark hole. Each time I woke up I was still groggy and tired. I'd glance around the room, at the chipped-away yellow paint showing the old bare wood on the ceiling, and at the streaks of red and white paint on the walls. It was old and musty and, like the rest of the house, I thought, should have fallen down years before. It took me a while to get it through my head. This old house was where I lived – permanently. Mom and I weren't going anywhere. The longer I stayed, the better the dark hole felt. I never wanted to wake up.

"I'll paint this old room," Martin told me. "You pick the colour."

Good idea. Sky blue, I thought at first, fresh, new, and light. It would help me mask the suffocated feeling that I was sure would kill me. But after a while I realized it didn't matter. Martin could put a hundred coats of paint on the walls and it wouldn't matter what colour – the room wasn't mine and never would be. I didn't know it in my brain so much as I felt it in my gut, that I was an intruder. I had intruded on Martin's and Luke's lives.

And the people who came around the house made me feel like I was intruding on their place, just like every other damn white person in history. The reserve. (Get it? Reserved. No room. No wonder they didn't want to change the name.) First, there were Martin's friends – mostly old guys that came around and sat in the living room or kitchen, pop cans in their hands, laughing and talking loud. When I entered the room, a hush blew over everyone as if they had been telling a secret and I wasn't in on it. Or maybe they were talking about me, although I doubted it. Why would they bother? Then they'd lean back in their seats and nod their heads and say stuff like, "Hey, Blondie," or "Who's the white girl?"

Then there was Luke, seventeen years old, very male, and all his very male friends. When I lived in the city I was used to guys checking me out, no problem. Even creeps, I knew what to do with them. I had a just-try-it attitude. I was the kind of girl who had a look for everyone. I could roll my eyes with the best of them. There wasn't a come-on line I didn't have a response for. But on the reserve I was off my game. I didn't know the rules. Luke was okay. When his friends weren't around he treated me normal – mostly he ignored me. But his friends would check me up and down

– their eyes crawled up my body as if they were wondering how I worked, if under my clothes my legs met at the same place as other girls' legs. They'd say, "Hey, what's up with you, Blondie?" or "Luke, man, where'd you get the little white girl?" I didn't know how to respond. Awkwardly, with two left feet and my fingers in my mouth, I'd head back to my room and lock the door behind me.

Even the little kids who came around looked at me weird. They'd stare at me as if their moms had forgotten to tell them it was rude to gawk. I'd check my nose for snot and my zipper to make sure it was pulled up. I felt like a freak. I wanted to say, "What the hell is there to look at, kid?" Then one day a boy about six came up to me, wiped his nose with the back of his arm, and said, "How'd you get so white?"

That was the beginning of the change that took place in my life. I started to realize that, on the reserve, white was something to stare at. White was different. I was different. Not good different. I felt like someone had let me into a private club for men only and I was a woman and now no one would let me out. I felt like I was at a party where people wore clothes and I had forgotten mine. People looked at me, but they didn't talk. I looked back at them and I didn't talk either. It got so that as soon as I saw someone coming, I locked my bedroom door and only came out when I absolutely had to.

If you think I was close to crazy, you are dead right. I was a head case. All I did was wish and wish, knowing there wasn't a thing I could do. I wished Mom would come to her senses. I wished I would wake up one day and Mom would say, We're going home – this was all a bad mistake. I wished I was in control, not Mom. My life was in her hands, and the thought terrified me. In all my experience with

Mom, I didn't remember her making one good decision. The truth was, Mom didn't make very many decisions at all. She was the kind of woman who let circumstances decide her fate. She could get her head around decisions like should she go to bingo or a movie. She could handle decisions like what we'd have for supper, Kraft Dinner or SpaghettiOs, but even there she narrowed the choices down to circumstance. She only bought a few groceries, so we ate the same thing night after night. When it came to decisions about what to do with her life, Mom let circumstance rule there as well. Forget school, she said. She was too dumb the first time, so why would she be any better the second? And she had a daughter to raise, so getting a job was out of the question.

When it came to looking after me, Mom pretty much left that up to talk-show paranoia. Afraid I'd be stolen or smuggled or raped or murdered or sold, she stuck to one answer – No – followed by a brief warning. That way she didn't have to make a decision. Can I go to the store? No, there are men lurking around the street corners. Can I get a bike? No, the roads are too busy. When I got to be around eleven or twelve, my social life took place on nights I could convince Mom to let me sleep over at Sarah's or Katy's house. And that was a lot, as many nights as they'd let me. Mom was okay with that; she deferred easily to other parents who she considered competent enough to take the blame if I disappeared or was murdered or something.

Katy told me once, in a seriously condescending voice, that she didn't want to hurt my feelings, but her dad had said he didn't mind me staying over because my mom was white trash and I could be more than that one day. I wasn't hurt – she hadn't told me anything I didn't already know.

By the time I was thirteen I would wait until Mom fell asleep, and then I'd sneak out the door. I'd get home by midnight or one and she didn't know a thing. That's when my social life really got going. I solved the problem of the "no" answer by never asking.

Once I was out on the reserve I was seriously trapped, sentenced to live with the consequences of Mom's one and only life-altering decision. The first real decision she'd ever made, as far as I knew, and the stupidest decision she could ever make. A nuclear-powered, blow-our-lives-into-smithereens kind of decision, and what could I do about it?

I covered my head with my comforter and thought up stuff I could do to make her realize she had made a desperate mistake. I thought about faking an illness. I dreamed up ways to get the doctor to tell Mom to take me back home.

"You have to move back to the city, for Josie. You have no choice," I imagined him saying. I feigned asthma and allergies and blew my nose and coughed and choked.

But I was never one for drama. My act was completely unbelievable and way too much work to keep up. I tried drawing to entertain myself. Forget it, I wasn't inspired. After I had drawn my bed, the windows, and the dresser a dozen times, I was bored and tossed my pencils and sketch pad under the bed. I slept most of July and August away, soaking up any comfort I could get from my mattress, sheets, pillow, and comforter, which were the only things other than a few clothes and pencils that belonged to me. Without my bed, I don't know what I would have done.

The other thing that kept me company – it might sound completely nuts to you – was an old Canadian flag in my bedroom window, thumbtacked at the corners and threadbare. Instead of the maple leaf in the centre it had a picture of an Indian warrior – camouflage fatigues, bandana, and all. He looked like he came right out of the '60s. There was something about the way he held up his fist that kept me going. When I was awake I imagined the warrior on the flag standing up in front of the government buildings, beating a drum and shouting protests. I wanted a little of his defiance, his obstinancy, but I felt like a wet sponge and he was probably dead by now. If he wasn't dead, then he would be an old man, as frayed as the flag, I figured. Worn out and faded, the way the sun had eaten the silky fabric, leaving the sorry warrior looking pale and used, his face old and weather-beaten. He would have given up years ago, because from what I had seen, it didn't look like the Indians had won any battles with Canada. From listening to Martin and his friends, it sounded like they must have lost whatever war they fought.

But that was when I was awake. It got so that mostly I was asleep. I'd be up around seven and back to sleep by ten in the morning, up and down again around noon, and then again in the afternoon. At suppertime I'd wake up for a few hours, then fall asleep again long before it got dark. Each day I got more and more tired. I was falling down a deep well and I kept on falling. There was no bottom. At first I didn't want to sleep so much, but after a while I didn't want to wake up.

The first day of school came, and Mom was right in a way – things did get better. It got me out of bed. I had no choice. I had to be at the bus stop at 7:30 in the morning.

Chapter 1

"Hey, Blondie."

Martin hunched over the kitchen table, one elbow on each side of his bowl.

"Sleep good?"

"Yeah."

"You always an early bird?"

"Yeah. Sort of." At least I used to be, when I didn't stay in bed all day.

"You hungry?"

"Yeah, sort of."

"You got anything else to say other than yeah?"

"Not really."

"There's mush on the stove. Get a bowl and a spoon."

"Thanks."

I slopped two spoonfuls of soft oatmeal into my bowl.

"Luke!" Martin hollered over his shoulder in the direction of the bedrooms. "Get your butt out of bed. You'll miss the bus.

"That lazy ass is never going to graduate if he doesn't figure out how to get out of bed in the morning," he said to me. "There was no sleeping in when I was a kid."

Martin grumbled a few more words into his bowl that I didn't hear. I filled my spoon with oatmeal and watched the porridge until I opened my mouth. If I didn't think about what it looked like – wet concrete – mush with brown sugar and milk didn't taste too bad. It was better than the dry, sugar-coated cereal I used to eat at home, which tasted like Styrofoam and cotton candy. And besides, warm porridge felt good sliding into my stomach.

"You like the mush?"

"Yeah."

"Me too. Ate it since I was a kid. Even when I was doing time."

I didn't ask Martin about doing time, partly because I wasn't too surprised. At first glance you could tell that he had probably been in a drunken brawl or two, and that the other guy had had a knife. The creases on his cheeks and chin, and lines that sliced into his leathery skin, said that he'd been through some heavy stuff. His forehead was gouged with deep purple scars that curved along the side of his left eye. It looked like someone had done some serious graffiti on his face.

But his face was like the way he talked – you got half the story and then were left to fill in the rest. Martin must have been a wide, muscled bouncer sort of guy when he was young and probably had an up-yours attitude that got him into trouble. He was still big for an old guy, although his shoulders kind of slumped forward and his belly was pretty round. And he still looked like he didn't care much about what people thought of him. I figured that if the guy with the knife got the worse end of the deal, it might explain the part about Martin doing time. But I couldn't ask him something like that. I couldn't say, "Where did you get those ugly scars on your face?" or, "Why did you do time?" I didn't even want to sit at the table with him, never mind ask him to tell me his life story.

"Finally got your lazy butt in here," Martin said when Luke entered the kitchen.

Luke ignored his dad's comment. He clasped one hand on the towel that was wrapped around his hips, while he grabbed the milk carton with the other and tipped it up to his lips. He opened his mouth like a seagull. Glug, glug, glug. Forget swallowing. It was as if there was an open drain from his mouth to his stomach.

I followed the path the milk would take – down his throat, into his gut – and was left with my eyes glued to his rippled abs, which were pulsing with each gulp. Instantly I was filled with a brand-new appreciation.

God – I caught my breath – he was hot. He was the kind of hot that melts your body fluids and sends chills up your spine at the same time. Where had I been? I hadn't noticed Luke in that way before. Not like that morning. But then, I'd never seen him almost naked. He looked like an advertisement for the ancient Greek Olympics. Put a laurel wreath around his head and I swear he'd have looked like Zeus or Hercules. He was taller than Martin and cut lean, like he was chiselled out of stone. His arms hung off his square shoulders with a casual, I'm-totally-in-control look. I did a quick mental check on whether my mouth was open. Then I lifted my finger to my lips just to make sure I wasn't slobbering. If Katy and Sarah could see what I was seeing, they would faint.

For a fleeting second I wanted to reach out and run my finger over his caramel-coloured, smooth, silky, almost hairless chest. Luckily I remembered that for some ridiculous and stupid reason the studly hunk standing in front of me was my brother, and that what was happening around the breakfast table was some outrageous thing called my new family. I grabbed my hand and held it down on my lap.

"You might as well finish that now," said Martin. "Your backwash too."

Luke licked his lips and wiped his arm across his chin. He tossed the empty milk carton into the garbage can, gulped a gut full of air, and let out a disgustingly gross wet belch loud enough to wake up Mom. Too much. Way too much. After spending the summer rolled in my comforter, I couldn't handle getting up in the morning and facing Martin and his small talk and Luke's naked body and garbage disposal burps.

"And put something on in the morning," said Martin, completely ignoring the burp. "Who wants to see your butt-naked gut at the breakfast table?"

"Good morning to you too, old man," Luke said. He threw his hand flat on Martin's back, knocking his father forward. "Good to see you're so bright this morning. And you, Blondie, how's it going?"

My head bobbed around as if it was on a swivel. Being broadsided by Luke's gorgeous body display sucked the air out of my chest. Words stumbled around in my throat, but the only sound that got to my lips was "Ugh."

Luke turned, retucked his towel, and sauntered back into his bedroom.

"You want any more?" Martin asked me as he spooned a second helping of oatmeal into his bowl.

"No. Thanks."

"You don't like it?"

"No. I like it."

I lifted my bowl and shovelled the rest of the cereal and milk into my mouth. I rinsed my bowl and left Martin sitting alone at the table as I headed to my bedroom. I shut the door behind me, slid the lock bar into its tunnel, leaned against the wall, and shimmied my back down until I was sitting on my heels.

Too frigging weird for words! How could Mom have done this to me? I wondered if she'd even clued in that there was a Luke. She was still pretty stuck on Martin, his snug-fitting jeans and his waltzing and the fact that he could make her laugh. It was pathetic.

I sunk my face in my hands. Who in her right mind has to grab one hand with the other so she doesn't reach out and fondle her own brother? Everything about this place creeped me out, and now I was creeping myself out.

Suddenly I had a thought. (Why had it taken so long?) Luke was not my brother, Martin was not my father, and the ramshackle, strange, and shabby house was not my home. The only reason I was there was because Mom had lost her mind and it hadn't returned to her yet. I was simply along for the ride because I had nowhere else to go.

I scrambled to my feet, yanked the closet door open, pulled out my old quilted suitcase, and tossed it on the bed. The zipper gaped open, waiting for my clothes and shoes. I stared at it and thought of what to do.

Phone Dad. The last time I had talked to him was about three years before. He told me he had found a new woman named Capricorn who made soap and organic cookies and taught belly dancing. They were moving up north to an island. He said I could come up and visit them as long as I found someone with a boat. So much for Plan A. Forget Dad.

Phone Mavis. The summer I was twelve flashed through my head, when Mom sent me east for quality time with her mom. Between bingo, poker, and sleeping half the day, she was too busy to hang out with me.

It must run in the family – the mother thing, I mean, or the non-mother thing. I first realized Mom was lacking something in that department when I met Sarah's mom. She worked at the university, attended lectures about the environment, and always had fresh-cut flowers on the kitchen table. She cooked with herbs and cream and made pasta from scratch. It was a whole mother thing I had never seen before. And she said she was going to change the world. "It's women's work," she said. "If we don't make this a better place for the children, who will?"

I wanted a mom like Sarah's, and I blamed Mom for being such a loser mother until I met her family. They all smoked loads of cigarettes, drank gallons of beer, and argued, a lot. Mom's sister Rena and brother Tracker lived with Mavis. Rena's kids were in foster homes because she was drying out, and Tracker didn't know where his kids were. With the bitch, he said. I guessed that meant their mother. The other sister, Henny, lived up the road with a little kid named Daisy. I think there was something wrong with the kid – she needed glasses or something – because she looked funny. She trailed behind her mother wherever she went, whining and snivelling, and Henny whined and snivelled back. I could hardly stand being in their company for more than a minute.

Okay, so scratch the Mavis plan. I plopped on the bed.

"Josie Jessop," I asked myself out loud in a totally pessimistic tone, "do you really think you are going anywhere?"

It didn't take me half a minute to get a clear answer. No matter how much I wished I was, I wasn't a gutsy teenager. I didn't know how to thumb my nose at life. I couldn't drum up a the-hell-with-it or take-off-anyway kind of attitude. I was your basic wimp.

"Hey, Blondie." I was jolted out of my thoughts by a loud rap on the door. "You coming?"

"Yeah."

"Then hurry up."

I grabbed my notebooks, stuffed them into my knapsack, tossed the suitcase into the closet, and slammed it shut. Luke waited at the top of the stairs and stepped aside to let me pass. Then he followed me out the door. The sun was bright and already warm. The sky was huge and blue with high white clouds. I was still embarrassed by my performance at breakfast, but the brilliant day cheered me up a little. Apart from the chirping of summer birds, a quiet rustle in the trees, and our shuffle, it was quiet – a weird country kind of quiet I wasn't used to.

But I got to thinking that really the moment was completely normal. I hustled along, keeping up with Luke's steps. It was a beautiful day and I was heading to the bus. Normal. Luke had his clothes on; I was inside my own skin and in control of the thoughts in my brain and the words in my mouth. Normal. As close to it as I'd been for months.

"You like this place, Blondie?"

Being out of the house brought on a few moments of unusual clear-headedness along with a spark of confidence. For an instant I became my normal self and forgot the lame-brain Josie who had developed over the summer.

I said, "You don't have to call me Blondie."

"You don't like it?"

"No."

"What about Jo Jo?"

"No. Gawd, no. That's worse."

"How come?"

"That's Mom. She won't quit with that J-J-J-o-o-o J-J-Jo-o-o thing. It's bad enough just Jo Jo, but she rolls the J around in her mouth like it's juicy and then sings the O until... well, until I feel itchy."

Luke laughed.

I slipped a look at him out of the corner of my eye. He was smiling like there was nothing at all unusual about what was happening. We were having an everyday conversation. I was talking, he was talking. I couldn't get a grip on it – it had been so long since I was a person.

"She probably thinks it's cute."

"Yeah, maybe when I was two."

"So what's it going to be?"

"Josie."

"Okay, Josie."

"Thanks."

"Sure you don't like Blondie?"

"Yeah, I'm sure."

"I don't mean it in a bad way."

"Yeah, I know. I just don't like it."

I wasn't at all sure whether he meant it in a bad way or not. When his friends said "Blondie," I'd catch them pausing or snickering as if I had missed a private joke. Which brings up blonde jokes. Before I moved to the reserve I thought they were funny. They were like moron jokes; anyone could be one. Since I'd been at Martin's it felt like blonde jokes were sent my way special delivery – like I had to sign the register to make sure they arrived and I got the point. Blonde jokes weren't about anybody these days but me.

As Luke's body moved through the air on the way to the bus, I caught a drift of the musky scent of men's cologne or deodorant. Suddenly I had a vivid memory of a recurring dream I had when I was a little girl. In the dream it was a hot summer day; I was four, maybe five years old and I had a big brother. Every dream was the same. I sat in a little frog pool, set on a thick uncut green lawn. I splashed while he held a hose and filled the pool with water. I remember waking up with the image of his wet body glistening in the sun. He had a toothy smile and a big hearty deep laugh. I remember wishing the dream were true. I secretly picked out boys at school, in books, at bus stops, or walking down the street who would be my brother. My imaginary surrogate brothers were always tall, dark, handsome boys who rode black horses, drove fast cars or chrome motorcycles. They walked like Luke, swinging their arms, confident, as if they knew exactly where they were going. Déjà vu. I'd been here before – only I think the last time I was asleep.

Luke and I didn't say any more as we followed the lane through the woods to a massive stand of oaks where the gravel road met the worn-out pavement. The road, just wide enough for one car, was gouged in places by giant potholes deep enough to shake loose a compact's tire. In less than five minutes we reached the bus shelter. Luke stepped inside, dropped his butt on one end of the bench, and stretched his legs along its complete length. I leaned against the door of the wooden shack.

"You want to sit down?" he said when he realized he hadn't left me any room.

"No, I'm good out here."

Outside, the front wall of the shelter was plastered with duct tape and notices, three or four thick, advertising bands playing at the youth centre, first-aid classes, soccer tournaments, birth-control workshops, elders' dinners and you name it. It got me thinking there must be a village nearby – something was happening somewhere.

The other walls were covered with paint and felt-pen graffiti inside and out. Messages had been carved into the slats with pocket knives or nail files. There were graphics: old and faded feathers, fists, fingers, scratched or painted one on top of the other. Some I could hardly figure out. Words were slashed across the old wood in gobs of thick paint: WARRIOR and RIGHTS and RED POWER and PEACE and LOVE. I thought about the flag. ROSE LOVES LUKE was neatly written with black felt pen and surrounded by a red heart. The ink was fresh. Underneath it were messages like ELSIE LOVES LUKE and ANDREA LOVES LUKE.

"You write this stuff?" I said.

"Huh?"

"You write this stuff on the bus shelter?"

"What stuff?"

Luke stretched his neck around the corner and peered at the wall.

"Looks like everyone loves you."

"Ah, shut up." He snickered and slumped back against the wall. "That's BS."

"Traci loves Desi too. Elsie loves you and Desi. Lesley and Maggie love Desi."

"Whatever."

Luke wasn't concerned. He had a look on his face that said, They all love me – so what?

I stumbled down a small incline around the side of the shack and into a shallow ditch lined with rocks and long, dried grass. Blackberry vines hooked my pant leg as I grabbed on to the backside of the shelter to steady myself. The back wall of the shack was less artsy than the front. It was like people headed around the back away from the road to say what they really thought. Under my fingers I could just make out the words WHITE PEOPLE SUCK. Every swear word and crude phrase I had ever heard, and some I hadn't imagined, were smeared across the boards. LAWRENCE FUCKED CARMEN AGAINST THE WALL 2001. I traced my fingers along the weathered boards. JESUS LOVES YOU was barely visible under the thick and deliberate black strokes of INDIANS RULE. Someone had pressed heavily with a blue pen and written a poem. The ink had dried up in places, so I couldn't read every word – *I wash up good, you take me out, I smile, I'm a good little girl, outside, inside out, watch me shout.* There was more – I wanted to stay and read it, but the bus lumbered around the corner and stopped in front of the shelter.

I hooked my pack on my back and staggered up the stairs of the bus in front of Luke. We were the first on the bus, so supposedly we could take our pick of the seats. Luke stepped around me and shot to the back, while I slipped into a seat a few rows behind the bus driver, an instinctive move that soon proved correct. When the bus picked up the rest of the kids from the reserve, every one of them walked past my seat except a skinny boy with glasses as thick as dinner plates. He plopped himself down, stared straight ahead, and didn't seem to notice the white girl sitting next to him, trying to be as inconspicuous as possible. We were a good pair. Two weirdos sitting together.

The bus bumped along the forested road and then sped down the highway past farms and fields toward school. My stomach flipped and flopped, barely kept in place by the lump in my throat that wouldn't go away. I felt eyes staring at the back of my head and wished I had worn a hat to cover up my blonde hair. The bus was the ultimate trap.

Forty minutes locked in a tin can with a bunch of kids I didn't know. What if they all ganged up on me? Or started telling white jokes? Luke was my only link to safety, and what the hell good would he be at the back of the bus with a sea of kids between him and me? Besides, I didn't know him well enough to depend on him.

I tried to distract myself by concentrating on the losers who sat near the front of the bus with me. I listened to a girl sitting in the seat in front talking to herself, a big guy across the aisle sucking air through his teeth like an old vacuum cleaner, and the boy with the glasses next to me, who kept opening his mouth and smacking his lips together as he chewed a big wad of bubble gum. So much for entertainment.

A boy's voice shot over the general rumble of voices in the back. "Hey, Luke, that your sister?"

"Yeah, man, what's with Blondie?"

God, just what I was afraid of. And I didn't hear Luke respond.

"Did ya hear the joke about the blonde, the redhead, and the Indian?" the first voice said.

Then I heard Luke pipe up. "Shut up, Chris. And her name's Josie."

And someone nearby said, "Can I sit down?"

A girl was standing in the aisle, leaning against the back of the seat. She had a saucer-shaped face and wide, round, glossy black eyes. She was short, with stocky shoulders and hips and thick thighs. Her hair was pulled tightly back into a ponytail with a razor-sharp zigzag diagonal part and her full lips were painted bright red. A tough but cute-looking girl. She hooked her butt on the corner of the seat in front of me beside the girl who was talking to herself. "Hey,

Shelley," she said when the girl didn't respond.

Shelley shoved her knapsack under the seat, turned sideways, and planted her feet in the aisle. The other girl turned and looked right at me.

"My name's Rose."

"Hi," I said. I was shocked by her attention, but unsure whether I should be flattered or afraid. There was nothing Superstore about the girl's clothes. Everything she wore was new, brand name, the latest, and expensive. There was something in the air around this girl that I could feel right off. She was somebody. Which brought up the question: Why would she introduce herself to me, the nobody white girl at the front of the bus? She looked honest, but the lump in my throat told me to be careful.

"I'm Josie."

"What grade you in?"

"Ten."

"Me too. Where you from?"

"The city. I've lived in the city, different places, since I was a kid."

"Yeah? Cool. It's not like around here I guess. I mean, the city."

"Yeah, I mean, no, really," I said.

She carried on talking. I slipped in one-word answers now and again, when it was absolutely necessary: really, yeah, wow. It's not that I wasn't interested in what she had to say – Gawd, I was dying for a decent conversation. She had caught me off guard. My whole summer had been spent with my mouth closed, avoiding everyone. Now I seemed to be a ditz, incapable of having an intelligent conversation. On top of being, still, suspicious. Why was she talking to me?

"Rose?" I said. "Did you say your name was Rose?"

"Yeah," she said.

Okay, I thought to myself, I get it now. The bus shelter. Rose loves Luke. Rose seemed to be the most recent instalment in Luke's love life. And I was Luke's stepsister – or something like that. So I get Rose's attention.

Chapter 2

Forget what Mom said about being fine once I got to school. School sucked. I felt just as out of place at school as I did at Martin's. Kids were grouped differently than they were in town. There were kids who walked to school, kids who drove their own cars or caught a ride with a friend, and kids who took the bus. The third group hung out in the corner of the school parking lot, waiting to come and go on the buses. Bus kids were separated into two subgroups: white kids and Indian kids. White kids hung around three buses parked near the back entrance to the school, and Indian kids stood in an area between a huge oak tree and the fence. The groups were so distinctly separated, it was as if a double yellow line had been drawn between them – no passing. Once in a while an Indian kid stood with the white crowd or the other way round, but rarely and not for long, and it was usually a girl, flirting. And then there was me – the group of one. The white girl waiting for the Indian bus. Talk about a twist. There wasn't even a sub-sub-subgroup for me.

And inside the bus there were rules as well that kept the groups in order. I didn't know exactly what they were, but after a couple of weeks I had figured out this much: Empty seats didn't necessarily mean you could sit down. Some seats were reserved for specific people. Even if there was no other seat and that person was in bed with pneumonia and ready to die, that empty seat was to stay empty. If you were lucky, a subtle lift of someone's eyebrow or tilt of someone's neck indicated a seat's designation; if not, you'd hear "Who the hell you think you are sitting in Vicky's – or Joe's or whoever's – seat?"

It didn't happen to me much. My instincts were good right from the start – in this, at least. There were some empty seats you could sit on without committing any infraction. Those seats were the first three or four rows behind the bus driver. The skinny guy with bottle-thick glasses, the girl who talked to herself, and the guy who was so big he needed two seats to himself were usually the only ones there. And me, of course, the one and only white girl.

Even though I wasn't sure what Rose was up to, I was glad she sat with me. We didn't talk at school, but at least she might make the bus rides more interesting. I hoped. Even if it was only because I was Luke's stepsister, it wasn't like I could afford to be choosy.

I leaned against the fence alone, trying not to feel like a complete loser. I *had* to cross the invisible double line, what choice did I have? Welcome to the group of Josie. I could hear the comments, like "Why the hell is a white girl getting on our bus?" and "What's with the honky chick?" and that was the tame stuff. When the bus door finally opened, the kids all started shoving, like there was something other than a boring ride home waiting for them inside.

I hung back, waited until the last kid filed onto the bus, and then I couldn't put it off any longer. Dreading the next forty minutes, I climbed the stairs and stood next to the driver, glancing around, hoping to find an empty seat. The girl who talked to herself came out of nowhere and staggered up behind me as the door shut.

"Hey, you," Rose said. She was sitting next to the window four rows behind the driver. She motioned to me with her purse. "Saved you a place."

Rescued. Just like I hoped. What a relief. I plopped next to her, leaving the girl standing alone talking to herself.

"It rained on the blackberries," she was saying. "The red ones aren't going to ripen." She scuffed her bag along the floor and stood gazing down the aisle. The bus was crowded, even the front seats. I glanced around to see where she would sit. Knapsacks were strategically placed, and kids sat with their knees up and their faces looking the other way. No way. Forget it if she wanted a seat. As the bus jolted forward, the driver hollered, "Sit down back there."

"Lots of red berries. They won't ever be blackberries." The girl stumbled. One knee fell next to me and her knapsack landed on my lap.

Rose turned around and said, "Move the hell over." Her voice was so loud that nobody would have missed what she said. The bus got quiet. "Can't you see that Shelley needs a seat?" she hollered.

Rose's eyes narrowed on the girl sitting behind us. The girl huffed, "Whatever," almost as loud as Rose. But she yanked her bag off the seat and made room for Shelley.

"There you go, girl." Rose pointed to the empty spot. "You got yourself a seat."

Shelley leaned over my body and stroked Rose on the face. "The blackberries got rained on. The red ones won't ripen," she said.

"They're good yet, Shelley. You pick some more and Mom will bag them up for the freezer. We'll jam them later."

Shelley rolled off me and stumbled into the seat behind. She looked at Rose and she nodded. A huge grin filled her face. She didn't seem to notice the girl's cold shoulder beside her.

Rose said in a matter-of-fact voice, "Shelley picks blackberries. She fills ice-cream pails and brings them around door to door. Ten dollars a pail. She probably makes a fortune."

"Really?" I said. I was stunned. Rose had played that seat scenario like she was a totally no-crap kind of girl.

"She's a Jackson. There's a few of them like Shelley," Rose added in the same straightforward voice.

I didn't know what to say about blackberries or Shelley, so I said, "Thanks for the seat."

"Yeah, no problem," Rose said. "Sorry I didn't rescue you earlier."

"Hey, that's okay. I'll get used to this eventually."

"How'd you get to school in town?"

"Walked five minutes and I was there."

"Must have been nice," said Rose. "The bus sucks. Especially the snots and the idiots. They think they really got something going on – like where they sit is some kind of little power struggle, who's who deal. They're just stupid. And half of them are my cousins."

"You know everyone?"

"You got that right. Since I was born."

"You always lived on the reserve?"

"Where else? I was born there. Mom didn't even make it to the hospital. She delivered me on the sofa in the living room."

"Cool."

"I've lived there ever since. Same house, same everything."

Rose's voice trailed off. At first she sounded proud, then as if she was having second thoughts.

"I've never really had a house," I said. "We've lived in apartments or basement suites all my life."

"I'm going to live in an apartment some day," she said, as if it was something to be ambitious about.

"Really? How come?"

"They sound so grown-up and modern. So stylish, so uptown. I can just imagine saying, 'This is my apartment.' It would be so cool."

Not exactly my experience of apartments. We lived in town all right, in at least five different buildings that I could think of immediately. None of them could be called modern or stylish. Sarah lived in a pretty cool condo, but me and Mom were your basic welfare tenants.

"They're okay," I said. A whiff of our last apartment blasted through my head. "As long as you don't mind the smell of puke or body odour or litter boxes."

"No way, that's gross," she said, her face instantly contorting, showing her disgust.

"And the trouble is, it's not your puke or body odour or kitty's litter box," I said.

She laughed. "Okay, so maybe they aren't all cool."

I had dreamed of living in a house, of saying, "This is my house." I thought a house meant you had a family, you owned something, and you belonged somewhere. Someday I was sure me and Mom would get out of our scummy apartment. But it hadn't been Martin's old dumpy house I'd imagined.

"How do you like the reserve?" Rose asked.

"I don't know much about it. I just stick around Martin's house and try to keep out of the way."

"How's that for you?"

"Okay."

Rose could tell from the sound of my voice that the word "okay" was loaded. Whatever questions were bubbling away inside her, she didn't ask.

I didn't want to tell her I hated Martin's place and that morning I had planned to pack my bag and run away. What could I say? I only live on the reserve because I don't have a choice – I have nowhere else to go, but if I did I'd be out of the reserve so fast it would make your head spin. If I had had the guts I would have told her that I felt like an illegal alien dumped in a foreign country. I would have said I was afraid that at any minute someone might tell us we had to leave, and at the same time I wished they would.

"How long you guys been at Martin's?" Rose asked.

"Since the wedding. I moved in the first week of July after Martin and Mom came home from their honeymoon."

"Ever walked around the reserve?"

"No."

"Want to?"

Walk around the reserve? Why? Why would I want to strut around as if I was on display? I imagined people pointing and staring like the kids who came to Martin's house. I thought of the comments I had heard from kids on the bus. How could I remain invisible if I paraded myself around the reserve? My brain got in a cramp. My main goal – to hide out – was colliding with my curiosity to find out about the place and my desperation to do something. And on top of that I was totally surprised and flattered that someone had invited me to go somewhere. At that moment it didn't really matter what I would be doing. Anything was better than nothing.

So I said, "Sure."

"How about this afternoon?"

"Cool. Thanks. Can we start at Martin's house? So I can tell my mom."

"Sure. We'll go from there."

Rose stared out the window. The questioning look dropped from her face as the scenery whizzed by. She must be seeing the same signposts, traffic signals, woods, gas stations, farms and barns, houses and driveways, that she'd looked at every day since she started school. It was me, now, who had a million questions piling up behind my closed mouth. For instance, what do kids do for fun on Friday night, stuck way out on the reserve? Are there any other white girls on the reserve? Are white girls *allowed* to walk around the reserve? But I couldn't get the words right, so I let the conversation go silent. The boring rumble of voices and the drone of the bus tires almost put me to sleep.

After a few minutes Rose leaned her mouth close to my ear and lowered her voice in a way that made me think she was telling me a secret. She said her mom was shocked Martin actually got married. Especially so quickly. No one even knew he had a girlfriend.

"What really shocked everyone was that Martin would marry a..." She hesitated, then blurted out, "White woman."

The words fell out of her mouth and landed with a dull thud like they'd hit thick rubber. Everyone was shocked that Martin had married a *white* woman. So now Rose was going to drag me around like some weird curiosity – oh, here's the *white* daughter of the *white* woman Martin married.

The bus jerked to a stop at the wooden bus shelter. Me and Rose were the only two left – don't ask me where Luke was. It was too late by then to change the plans. We were getting off the bus and she was coming over. Besides, in spite of what she had said, there was something about her I liked. I thought that, given another time and without all the white girl, Indian reserve crap, we could be good friends.

"Hey, Mom," I said when we entered the living room. "What's up?"

Mom butted her cigarette in a bowl and squinted at the TV through the last puff of smoke.

"You gotta hold on there, Blondie. The world is turning and Lenore can't miss it," Martin said with a laugh.

He was sitting at his carving bench whittling yellow cedar. The floor was covered with curls of wood, as if he had spilled a bucket of popcorn. The scent of cedar cut through the musty smoke odour of Mom's cigarettes, leaving a peculiar acid smell in the room. Martin carved model canoes with little men or women sitting inside holding paddles. He sold them to shops in the city and art collectors. He was working on one about three feet long with eleven paddlers that was already sold to a museum somewhere.

"Hey, Rosietoes," he said. He threw her a big grin when she came into his view. "What's going on with you? Long time no see."

"Yeah, haven't been around for a while."

"You met Blondie, I see."

"Yeah, I'm taking her for a tour of the rez."

Martin laughed. "Tour guide, are you? Checking out the sights? Careful when you get down around Tina's place. She bites."

"No doubt," Rose said. "Her dogs aren't so special either."

Martin put his knife on the table, leaned back, and crossed his foot over his knee. He looked at Rose's face when they talked like they were old friends. There was something unusual about their conversation I couldn't put my finger on exactly.

"How's your mom?" Martin asked.

"Good," said Rose. "Working as usual. How's your mom? She broke her hip, didn't she?"

"Yeah." Martin shot a quick glance at Mom before he answered. "She's good now."

"Oh great," Rose said. "Is she home from the hospital? Can I see her?"

"Uh, no," Martin lowered his voice and turned his back toward Mom, who was so entranced by her soap opera that she wasn't paying any attention. "She's still in the hospital."

"No way," Rose said. "I bet she hates that. When's she coming home?"

"Soon," Martin said slowly as he flicked his eyes over his shoulder at Mom. "I hope."

Rose got the hint that Martin didn't want to talk about his mom, at least not if my mom was listening, and quickly changed the subject. I got the feeling I was missing something. I had met Martin's mom once in the summer, but no one said anything about her coming home or even where her home was. Rose made it sound like Martin's place belonged to his mom. And Martin made it look like he didn't want Mom to know what was going on.

Their conversation didn't stop there. Rose told him about someone who had been taken to the hospital during the night; he broke his neck, he might not make it. She was newsy – Rita won a car at the casino, Judy won $1,000 at bingo, the youth club was fundraising so they could renovate the building. I was surprised by the way they spoke to each other. They didn't talk like a teenager to an adult or a parent to a kid. They spoke face to face, eye to eye, as if they were both interested in the same thing. Their conversation made me wonder if I had ever had a real conversation with an adult.

"You're going where?" Mom perked up when a commercial interrupted her show. "Jo Jo, where did you say you're going?"

"Afternoon, Mom. Glad you're in the room," I said. I put on a voice like I was joking and then suddenly felt sad. I had never talked with Mom face to face. We didn't share anything like Rose and Martin. Never had. At that minute I ached to have Mom on my side, even if we could just be aliens together, but she was from a completely different planet than everyone, even me.

"We're going for a walk around the reserve," I said.

"What are you going to do?"

"Walk."

"Where?"

"Around the reserve."

"Why?"

"Mom! Lay off!"

Her back shot up board straight when she turned her head toward us. Her eyes bugged out watery and red from the smoke and TV. She was cornered and confronted. She recoiled with a look on her face like a cat in a barrel.

"Martin."

"Yes, Lenore," Martin said as if he was coaxing her out of the corner.

"Jo Jo wants to go for a walk around the reserve."

"I heard, Lenore."

"Well, I. . . " Mom looked away and reached for another cigarette. Half sentences were another one of Mom's trusty, noncommittal techniques. I fell for it and so did her friends.

She would start the sentence and then, in order to avoid making a decision about how to end it, she would leave the last word hanging in the air like a bat on a tree.

Martin had only known Mom a few months, but he knew her well enough not to finish her sentences. "You what, Lenore?" Martin said.

"Nothing," Mom said. She nervously lit another cigarette.

There was a blank spot in the conversation. When Mom was uptight, if someone didn't finish her sentences they just got left unfinished with her sitting there wondering what happened.

"Are you worried the Indians will get your little girl?" Martin said, in a way that made it hard to tell whether he was serious or joking.

Rose folded her arms across her chest and lifted her jaw in Mom's direction. She wasn't joking. And I got a lump in my stomach that told me there wasn't anything funny going on in the room. A line was being drawn, and I wasn't sure which side I was on. I wanted to support Mom, who was about to fall into the hole she was digging. I was her daughter; we should be on the same team and I knew it. But I also knew where she was headed and I didn't want to go there. And what was I going to do with Rose? If all hell broke loose – and only I knew what it was like when Mom went ballistic – I would have to deal with Rose.

"No. No, but. . . " Mom's eyes glassed over.

"But what?" Martin leaned his head back into his clasped hands.

"But we might be dangerous?" Rose snapped.

O God, leave her alone.

Martin looked at Rose and choked back a laugh. "Lenore, sweetie. Don't worry. It's only Monday. The Indians aren't too wild this early in the week."

The corner of Mom's eye twitched and she tightened her lips. Mom didn't usually pick up subtleties in conversations, but she knew Martin was making a joke at her expense. Not good. She held herself together, and after a moment she said, "That's not it." But that was exactly it. She was afraid of the reserve, of Indians, but she had no words either for her feelings or that were fit for the situation. And she had curled up in a ball in her imaginary corner.

I stood near the stairs on one point of a triangle. Mom was on the sofa making a second point, and Martin and Rose were situated on the third point. I wanted to close ranks with Mom. She needed me to rescue her from herself. I knew how she felt, but I disagreed with her at the same time. Alien. That was the word she was looking for. She wanted to ask whether aliens like her daughter were safe and welcome and okay on the reserve. I wanted to say it for her, but I hated what Mom thought about Indians. And now we were faced with it flat out.

Mom had argued with Mavis about Indians on the phone, two weeks before the wedding. Mavis obviously had told Mom you couldn't mix oil and water. I imagined her voice: "It'll never work. And furthermore, you should think about Josie. The Indian reserve is no place for her."

"You're prejudiced," hollered Mom.

Of course Mavis must have denied it.

"What do you think?" Mom said in a controlled voice. "You think Indians are slinking around the corners of the reserve waiting to pounce on a little white girl?" (How was that for irony?)

I didn't hear Mavis's response, but it was what Mom said next that made me understand the trouble she was in now.

"Anyway, Mom," she had said, "Martin isn't wild and stupid and drunk like all the other Indians. He's different."

No wonder we were locked in the house and never went anywhere. Mom was suffering the consequences of her non-existent decision-making skills. When she decided to marry Martin, she had forgotten to think about actually living on a reserve, where there would be no one else around except Indians. Hello, Mom, what were you thinking? "One good Indian" was what she was thinking. One good Indian with a great butt in a pair of GWG jeans who knows how to dance. Can you imagine? That's as far as Mom had thought. She loved Martin, and other than that she was afraid and suspicious and who knows what else. And at that moment even Martin wasn't on her side.

Mom opened her mouth to explain. No words came. She looked helplessly at Martin. Sensing the impossibility of the situation, she gave up, turned her head back to the TV, and stared at a fast-food commercial.

After a few moments she said, in a voice we could barely hear, "Okay, but don't be too long."

Gradually the pressure leaked out of the room like air from a balloon with a pinhole. Rose loosened her grip around herself and leaned back against the wall.

"We'll be home by five or so," she said. "Don't worry, Mrs. Angus. I'll take care of Josie."

"Yeah, don't worry, Mrs. Angus, Mrs. Angus," Martin parroted and then laughed loudly. He was still trying to make a joke out of it – to get the tension out of the room. "That sounds pretty good, eh, sweetie? Mrs. Angus."

Mom was on the edge of crying, but she shrugged her shoulders without looking.

Chapter 3

My conversations before I moved to the reserve were normal: I talked, my friends talked, I answered, they answered, you know, like a natural flow. My conversations after I moved to the reserve were stop and start. I was constantly holding my breath, waiting for a safe time to let the air out. I was in a steady state of alert, worrying, wondering, watching, and reworking everything I said, asking myself, "How bizarre do I feel so far?" I was walking on Mars and never knew from one step to the next whether the ground would be quicksand and suck me under or whether it would be thin ice and crack. I couldn't trust my feet either. Would they step out in the wrong direction, bump into things, step when they should stop, stop when they should step? They no longer seemed to be connected to my brain. I constantly felt like I was stubbing my toe. My instincts, the stuff I had always relied on, basic who's who and what's what kind of stuff, couldn't be trusted. And people's responses to the simplest things, things I had never questioned, like walking down the street, were now complicated and confusing.

Once we turned the corner, Rose shook like a wet dog. Her eyes brightened and a wave of lightness washed over her. She said, "Okay, which way do you want to go? Up the hill or down?" She laughed like she had forgotten Mom and what was said back at the house. "I've never done this before. A tour of the rez. Crazy."

"You decide. It's all new to me," I said. I didn't know whether I should look or not look. Should I walk down the street as if I'd done it a thousand times? Should I really check out the place and ask questions? I glanced around as inconspicuously as possible. The ditches were strewn with bottle caps and labels and empty pop cans that must have been thrown from passing cars. Off to the side the dusty woods, brittle grasses, dried leaves, and other signs showed that summer was over – stuff I had never noticed before. There were blackberry bushes everywhere and the air was sweet with the smell of rotting berries. It wasn't the city – there was no doubt about that.

Up ahead the road narrowed and the trees bent together, blocking out the late afternoon sun. Through the tunnel of forest I saw the steel grey water of the bay and heard the seagulls and surf. I was shocked. How could I have been locked away in that old house all summer and not even known the beach was only minutes away?

"My favourite place is up ahead. Clam Cove. This is where I come to think. It's awesome," said Rose.

She smiled and took a deliberate breath of the cool air.

"Feel that?" she said.

I copied her, sucking in the salt air until my lungs were so full they hurt and my head was spinning. We arrived where the sand met the road and faced the water, letting the salty wind snap at our faces. Way too much nature for me.

The beauty of the place took me by surprise. I had never taken much notice of scenery. It was boring. But this place was awesome. Two points jutted out into the water, making a deep U shape that looked as if a fist had scooped out a massive handful of shore. To the left, logs were scattered over a speckled surface of broken clamshells. To the right the cove was lined with broad, leafy maple trees. A heavy rope swing hung over the water.

Rose sat on a log and motioned to me to sit beside her. She closed her eyes as if she was meditating.

"This is Clam Cove," she said.

So this is what you do on the reserve. I imagined kids swinging and swimming in the summer and Rose sitting on the logs, sifting through the pebbles. I thought of the mall, the parking lot behind the grocery store, and the video arcade in town, places I retreated to when I needed to get away. I remembered holding my breath until cars turned off their engines or pulled away out of range. Suddenly the city seemed a little bleak and slightly desperate. The beach was peaceful and the skin on my face stung as if it was the first time it had ever felt real air.

"Nice place."

"This is my first-up, number-one spot on the tour."

"There must have been zillions of clams."

"Still are. We dig them when it's the season," Rose said. "It's a lot of fun. When the season opens we go out after it's dark and dig until midnight. You should come."

I said, "Sure." But I thought, Enough already. The place is beautiful, but that'll be the day, when I dig clams at midnight or even want to.

We got up and walked along the beach past the maple tree and the rope swing. Then we climbed up the bank and over a midden, which Rose said was a garbage dump from their village hundreds of years ago.

"University people love it. They come around every summer and dig up arrowheads and clamshells. Looking for the secrets of our past, I guess," Rose said, with a look as if to say she thought it was a waste of their time. "In another hundred years they'll be sifting through pop cans, rubber tires, and tampons."

We climbed up the bank, through the trees, and into a clearing. I saw a village off to one side and a rocky hill on the other. The hill was dotted with houses placed randomly between low, scrubby bushes, green fields, driveways, and cars. There were large buildings and a soccer field. We passed old houses and sheds and cars with wheels and no wheels and cars jacked up on wooden blocks with hoods or no hoods. There were no hedges separating one house from another, no lawns marking one property from the next. There were no fences or sidewalks. The houses weren't lined up facing the ocean. Some faced the water, others had their backs to the view. The place looked like someone had taken a bunch of houses and bushes and cars and driveways and other stuff and shaken them up in their hands like dice, maybe blowing on them a couple of times for good luck, and then thrown them onto the ground. Where the stuff fell, that's where it stayed. Not a lot of planning went into that village.

I had an urge to straighten it up, plant lawns, move cars, cut grass, and chop down the blackberry bushes. Suddenly I became agitated. How can they live like this? Don't they have anybody making rules about building houses and roads and parking cars?

"Welcome to our village," Rose said. She waved her arm in a semicircle. She kept her eyes on mine, waiting for my reaction. I tried to mask my mental disorder and annoyance with a blank stare.

"This is where most of us live. A few people like Martin and Luke live around the edges. And," she said with a drawl, as if I was on an official tour, "the community centre is that way." We turned and walked up a slight grade in the street toward the buildings.

After a while I realized there was nothing really extraordinary about the village at all. It looked old and poor, aside from a fancy new building with giant posts and beams and totem poles. But there were houses, cars, old pavement with potholes and flattened-out speed bumps – probably the same sort of thing you would find in any village. It wasn't landscaped, but there were fields and bushes and trees.

Still, it was like nothing I had ever seen before. I began to think it looked exotic. Not glamorous, alluring exotic. More like strange, foreign exotic. Third World country exotic. Like pictures I had seen in *National Geographic*. I just hadn't expected it in Canada, only forty minutes from town.

The street, if you could call it that – it was more like a driveway – was barely wide enough for two cars to pass. Off to the sides, at the ends of what looked like gravel driveways, stood short posts topped with painted signs saying Joe Road, Sam Road, John Road. As if everyone got their own road.

Rose caught me eyeing the small weatherbeaten sheds with no windows sitting behind most of the houses. They were the shape of chicken coops but tall, at least ten feet – too big to be outhouses and too small to be tool sheds.

"So you're wondering if we've got indoor plumbing around here?" she said. She had a serious tone to her voice.

I said, "No, not exactly," although the thought had crossed my mind.

"They're smokehouses. That's where the men sit around

at night and smoke a pipe and shoot the crap." Rose looked me square on as she described how the old men would sit in a circle and pass around a pipe filled with a secret dried grass found only on their sacred mountain, this with a lowered voice and a wave of her hand toward the bluff beyond the village.

"Oh," I said in a respectful voice. "Wow." I imagined smoke filtering out between the slats in the tiny sheds as the old men squinted, red-eyed and stoned.

Then Rose cracked up. "Just kidding," she said. "That's where we smoke fish. Almost every family's got one."

I laughed too. Very funny. You got me. I felt a little wounded and confused and pretty careful about what I should say next. I started to keep my eyes down and pretty much got a tour of my feet scuffing along the road.

I glanced up when we passed kids and adults coming and going on the road and in their driveways. Rose threw them all a wave that looked like she was swatting flies. Everyone returned exactly the same movement back to her as if it were scripted and practised, a secret motion passed between the initiated. They were all smiles when they saw Rose, but it was a different story when they noticed me. As soon as their eyes turned my way they either looked away or gave me a what-the-hell-are-you-doing-here look. I tried not to pay attention and concentrated on my running shoes. When a car pulled past us, the driver stuck his head out the window and threw Rose a high-five, then scanned me up and down. He was so deliberate he looked like he was nodding his head. I was new in town, I was white, I had blonde hair, you name it. There was something for everyone to have against me and they made it as plain as day.

"Hey, Charlie!" Rose called out to a little boy who was

yanking up his sweatpants and gawking at me with his mouth open. "You better find the string to those there pants or you're going to lose them.

"And you, Angel!" she hollered to a young girl who was sitting on the front stair next to the boy. "Tell your sister we are going to kick her butt in soccer this weekend."

Rose said something to everyone – kids, teenagers, old people were all treated the same. I thought about the city and Sarah and Katy. Other than our parents, we didn't speak to anyone who wasn't our age. Not unless we had to, like when the police strolled by, or a teacher. We ignored the little kids and avoided adults whenever we could. And really old people? Forget it – they were a different species.

"Here's our great city centre. If you look straight ahead you will see our community offices. To the left is our health station." Those were the new buildings that didn't look anything like the others – they were awesome. Again Rose feigned the voice of a tour guide, trying to lighten up what was becoming a pretty tense afternoon. It wasn't only me who could tell that most of the people weren't too pleased to see me. I think she was beginning to decide the tour hadn't been such a good idea after all. I don't know what was worse for her, showing me to the reserve or showing the reserve to me. Either way, she wasn't having a whole lot of fun. But she wasn't going to give up on it either.

"And, Josie Angus," she continued, "behind that incredible building," she pointed to the health centre, "is our new and soon-to-be-improved youth centre. At which, if you hang around long enough, you are sure to meet some of our hunky men."

She spoke in an exaggerated tone, pasting her humour on top of the awkwardness we both felt. I went along with her. I stuck a smile on my face too and copied her weird voice.

"First, Rosietoes," I said, emphasizing her nickname to make sure she knew I was joking, "I'm not Josie Angus. I'm Josie Jessop. And I'm never going to be Josie Angus."

Her face muscles loosened and she tossed me a real smile. "Just kidding. First, Josie Jessop," she copied me, "I'm not Rosietoes. At least not to you and hopefully not to anyone else in my semi-adult life."

She turned toward me and her voice got serious. "I have the totally grim feeling that I will be Rosietoes around here until the day I die. Do me a favour? Call me Rose."

I told her I knew how she felt. I explained about my nickname Jo Jo, how Mom wouldn't give up on it, how I hated the way she said Jooooo Jooooo all syrupy. Rose laughed. "That's a bad one," she said. "I'd hate that too." Then I told her that I felt uncomfortable when people called me Blondie. I talked about Martin and Luke and their friends, how I could never tell for sure whether they meant the name as an insult or what. She looked kind of confused for a few seconds and then said she had never thought of that and she could understand how that must feel. For a few moments Rose and I were just two girls walking down the street like normal teenagers, side by side without an ocean of misunderstanding separating us.

"Josie Jessop," she giggled, exaggerating the name, "here we are at the Hummingbird youth centre. Named after the mighty hummingbird. That's supposed to be a little inspiration for us troubled teenagers. You know, the thing about great things coming in small packages."

The youth centre was two old construction trailers butted up against each other, with a few additions tacked onto the sides. It was painted green and red with an Indian motif of a hummingbird painted in black on one corrugated tin wall We stepped into a large room lined with computers. Three kids sat with their backs toward us facing the screens. The sound of video games and rap music blasted through the building.

"I hang out here once in a while," Rose said. "It was better before they bought the computers. Now it's mostly computer freaks and video-game junkies. They sit here all day and gawk at the screen. Look at them – they don't even know anyone's in the room."

She raised her voice and one young boy turned his head slightly in our direction, raising his hand in a limp-wristed wave.

"Hey, Kenny," Rose said and then hissed, "Geeks," through her teeth.

In the kitchen she opened a bag of juice crystals, poured some into two glasses, and filled them with tap water.

"Here." She handed me the drink.

She picked up a saucepan off the stove and looked at two bloated wieners floating in grey, greasy water. "Supper's ready," she said with a disgusted voice. "For some species." She screwed her nose up. "It doesn't look like human food."

"Hey, what's up with you?"

A boy brushed past my arm and filled a glass with water. He opened his mouth and emptied the glass without swallowing, exactly as Luke had done earlier. Then he held on to his gut and let out a belch. Lovely. When you are raised in a house with just your mom and that's it, no guys, their habits come as a surprise. On one hand, their body odours and sounds completely disgusted me. On the other hand, some of the things guys did totally fascinated me. I imagined opening my mouth and pouring juice directly into my stomach and thought I would probably choke to death. It's like guys had to go after everything in a big, loud, smelly, wet sort of way, or something like that. Whatever it was, I was getting a crash course in living with men whether I wanted it or not.

"Who've you got with you?" the guy asked Rose. He lifted the bottom of his T-shirt and wiped his mouth.

"Josie," Rose said. "Haven't you met her yet?"

He said, "Not yet. I'd'a remembered Blondie."

"*Josie*," Rose said, as if she was correcting his grammar. "This is *Josie*, Luke's new stepsister."

"You mean *she's* the white chick who's *living* here?" he said. He looked at me as if I had landed from another planet.

"Yeah," I said. Get over it, I thought. I wanted to scream, What's the big friggin' deal?

"Yeah, she's *living* here." Rose must have read my mind. "So what?" Then she turned and said, "And Josie, this is Desi, Mr. Jock Man."

So this was Desi. A name that came up a lot between Luke and his friends. Desi was the guy who was selected for the national soccer team. And from the writing on the bus shelter, it looked like almost as many girls loved Desi as Luke. I could see why. He was as cute as Luke – and he wasn't my brother. Get over his attitude and he would have been a real hunk.

"Say hi to Luke for me, Blondie."

Before the reserve, when I was sure of myself, I would have flung my hand out and thrown him a flirty punch. I would have had a brilliant, sassy response ready for him in an instant. But I had turned into a boring dud, tired and disoriented. The Josie Jessop I used to know had lost her rhythm, and now she stood on wobbly knees, brain-dead, with nothing witty or smart to say.

"Josie," I squeaked and watched him walk out the door. I hoped he didn't hear me.

Rose continued the tour off the main road and up a snaky path covered over by blackberry bushes, which ended at an old tumbledown shack no bigger than Martin's living room. The wooden walls were weathered the colour of steel and leaned so far to the right they looked like they would collapse in the slightest wind. Thick clumps of moss covered the brown-red shingles on the roof, which dipped in the centre like a hammock. Tattered lace curtains hung on the broken, warped wooden windows. Through a door standing slightly ajar, I could see a broken-down table and a three-legged chair leaning against the wall.

I started to wade through the long grass to look inside, but Rose held her arm across the path in front of me and stood back. She said it was her grandfather's house and she had run up the path to visit him every day until she was five years old.

"He had a raspy old voice and his house smelled like duck soup," she said. "He used to reach his arms out when he saw me coming, and I would run and jump on his lap."

Rose watched the shack silently as if she expected someone to appear. An image of an old man flashed into my mind. He had red suspenders and white hair springing out around the sides of his ball cap and over his ears. He was shrunken in his old age and bent. Rose turned and began to walk back toward the road. I took a quick glance over my shoulder. Baked oak leaves swirled in an eddy through the long grass next to the front door. Then suddenly it was still. I caught a waft of something greasy and meaty and then a faint hint of smoke as I followed Rose down the path. I kept checking back to see if someone was there.

"This," said Rose. We were standing in a field off to the side of the path. "This is the exact spot where my family had its big house." She told me that there used to be a row of long cedar houses along the beach. Each extended family in the village had a big house with heavy mats partitioning off sections for couples and their children.

"Sort of like a great big apartment," she said. "Except that everyone is your family."

"Pretty weird," I said. "Family's pretty big around here, I guess." The idea got my brain stuck. "My family's just me and Mom."

When I said it like that it sounded so empty. For one thing, I don't think I ever thought about me and Mom as being family. It wasn't much to think about. I guess Mavis and them out in Winnipeg were family, but not like what Rose was talking about.

"Are you kidding?"

"Well, Mom hates her mom, who I call Mavis so she doesn't have to be reminded that she's a grandma. And her dad took off when she was a kid. My dad did the same thing."

"No way. So it's you and your mom and that's it?" Rose said. "You got cousins?"

"Yeah, in Winnipeg, but I've only seen one of them. Once." And she was pretty weird, I said to myself.

"That's *so* strange. I got forty-two cousins, last I counted, and most of them live around here," she said. "There may even be more. I can't keep up with Uncle Wayne. He's got babies younger than his grandbabies."

"Really?"

"Yeah, really. And my grandma is proud of every one of

them. The more grandchildren the better. She says she is a wealthy woman because she counts her riches in grandchildren."

I couldn't imagine. Mavis said she would let us know when she wanted to be Grandma and don't hold our breath. Right now, she said, she was going to have a life and she wished her family would leave her alone. She didn't seem to care that her grandchildren were in foster homes somewhere or living with "the bitch." She didn't care about me either, for that matter.

No wonder I didn't think about family much. Suddenly I felt like an orphan. I didn't have anybody.

Rose said, "Now my cousins are having babies." Confused by the empty look on my face she laughed. "Babies, babies, babies. Around here they are the best thing. Everyone wants babies."

"Wow."

I liked how Rose's family sounded. I thought about meeting Martin's mom. She had told me to call her Grandma, and it felt good. Maybe if she did move home I could have a Grandma like Rose.

Rose's house backed onto the field. It looked exactly like Martin's, only green. I was relieved no one was home. As I waited for Rose to find a jacket I looked at the checkered linoleum floor, the walls covered in school pictures, the sheet-like curtains tacked to the windows. Everything was exactly like Martin's house. Did everyone on the reserve have the same kind of house?

As if she'd read my thoughts, Rose said, "It's a rez house. Seen one, seen them all." She said something about the houses in the subdivision being bigger and newer and then added, "It all must look pretty odd to you."

"I've just never been on a reserve before," I said.

"Hey, well, you're on one now," Rose said. "We'd better get going."

Walking back through the tunnel of trees towards Martin's place, it felt as if the Josie Jessop I once knew was fading away. I couldn't get a grip on her. I remembered her like she was someone I had met and known for a day or two. My body was the same, it was cold and covered in goosebumps from the cool damp air. But now it was the subject of a scientific experiment: lift a perfectly normal girl from a perfectly normal life, set her in a completely foreign and weird place, get people to look at her like she's weird, get people to treat her weird, watch her and test her response. Watch her question everything she knew to be true and doubt her very existence. Record how long it takes for her to go completely out of her mind.

I wanted to leave Rose in the woods, run to Martin's house, grab Mom and our clothes, and thank Martin for his trouble. I would tell him the experiment didn't work. Mavis was right after all; you can't mix oil and water. I would tell him to post a sign on the reserve – "White-free zone" – that would warn all us unsuspecting white people to stay away. Mom and I would drive home to our apartment and I would phone Sarah and Katy and go to the mall. Like normal.

One thing I had got perfectly clear from my tour of the reserve was that I wasn't welcome there. Even the little kids had a what-do-you-think-you-are-doing-here sort of expression on their faces when they looked at me. I glanced at Rose out of the corner of my eye and I could tell she knew it too. She scuffed her heels and breathed heavily as she walked, as if trying to make up for the failure of conversation between us. For a while on the bus that morning, and again that afternoon, we had crossed the ocean. We had spoken and listened and laughed and understood each other. Girl to girl, across culture and colour, we had had our ten minutes of fun. But now that the afternoon was over and there was nothing more to say, the only thing we shared was the space between us. She was over there, I was over here, or the other way around, and there was a giant space between us. A great big ocean and forget about crossing it.

Rose met my eyes square on, and I knew she knew; our separate places were carved even deeper now – not what she had intended as the outcome of the tour. She had something to say to me, I was sure. She had swallowed her anger with Mom, but she hadn't forgotten it. And now she saw the other side – that her people didn't like me – plain as day.

Luckily she didn't ask me if I liked the reserve. What would I have said? It was strange, messy, unorganized, and everyone looked at me funny? Would I tell her I felt like a total alien and that I wanted to run away, go home, if only I had a home to go to?

"Thanks for the tour."

"No problem. I guess it's kind of different?"

If I tried to reach out and touch Rose I would have been sucked into the ocean that separated us and drowned. I said, "No – it's – it was really great to see where you live. And the village."

"No problem," she said again. "See you tomorrow."

When she disappeared around the corner I sat on the edge of the front porch and leaned against the Harley that Martin was going to fix when he got around to it. My face turned hot and swollen and my eyes clouded over with stinging tears. My life sucked. Grade ten was supposed to be great – guys, dances, parties, shopping. I had planned to get a job so that I could have my own spending money. Well, I'd got the picture of my new life today. On the reserve there were no grocery stores, gas stations, or coffee shops. There were no guys interested in me, no parties that I knew of, no mall. And the damn Pacific Ocean separated me from my only potential friend.

Mom was glad I was home. At least she lifted her head from watching TV long enough to throw me a pinched, squinty smile through a cloud of smoke. I welcomed the sooty smoke smell. It was familiar, and I needed that.

"What's for supper?" I blurted out, a question from the past, whose answer had always been "Go make something for us both, would you, dear?" But instead Mom shrugged, and I heard Martin clanging pots in the kitchen. This much had changed between us: Martin cooked and cleaned instead of me. Fine with me. I headed to my room and slid the lock closed, wrapped myself in my comforter, and flopped on the bed.

I woke up to a rat-like scuffling noise coming from under the bed. I lifted my head to clear the sleep out of my ears, and the noise got louder in the direction of the heat vent. It wasn't the familiar wheeze and chug of the furnace or the crackling of the vents cooling down. Someone or something was moving downstairs or just outside.

I pulled myself out of bed and wiggled out on the window ledge until the sharp edges cut into my hip bones. From there, I peered down at the basement window, expecting to see or hear someone. The window was boarded up and painted with graffiti, just like the matching one around the front. I pulled myself back inside and stood at the foot of my bed. I closed my eyes and listened to the scuffling noise again. I must have been standing right on a furnace duct, although no air was shooting through, because I felt heat from the floor on my soles and then my ankles and then right to my knees – soft bubbly heat that made my legs weak. Then suddenly the noise disappeared and my legs were freezing. I stood still for a few moments, trying to find a logical explanation.

"Supper," I heard Martin holler from the kitchen.

Nothing logical about that, I said to myself. Crazy.

Luke was already sitting at the table, heaping his plate with meat and vegetables. "Got any more of this deer?" he asked.

"Yeah," Martin said. "Leave some for Blondie."

I sat down between them, opposite Mom, spooned mashed potatoes onto my plate, and covered them with gravy. Dinner noise was the sound of forks and knives clinking. With Luke chewing on one side and Martin chewing on the other, I had to concentrate on the inner-ear noise of swallowing my potatoes to avoid being completely grossed out. Out of the corner of my eye I noticed that Luke ate meat and potatoes like he drank milk. He shovelled huge mounds of food into his mouth and then with one seagull-like motion it was thrown into his stomach. No need for teeth. In no time at all he emptied his plate and filled it up with another equally huge pile.

"Heard you had the grand tour of the rez," he said, mouth full of food.

I kept my eyes on my plate to avoid Luke's disgusting chewing and talking combination act.

"Yeah."

"So what do you think?"

"It's a nice place."

"What did you see?"

"The beach, houses, the youth centre," I said.

"You meet anyone?"

"Yeah."

"Who?"

"I don't remember." I tried to make my voice sound interested. "Oh yeah, some Desi guy."

"Sounds like you loved the place."

I guess I didn't do a very good job of concealing my feelings. Luke laughed and continued eating.

I'd had enough potatoes, gravy, and conversation so I stood up and rinsed my plate and stacked it in the sink.

"Thanks for dinner, Martin."

When I got back to my room I was in no mood to stay there. But there was nowhere to go. Outside on the reserve I was just as much of an alien as I was with my new nutso family. I lifted the warrior flag, folded my arms on the windowsill, and stared into the backyard. It was a clearing the size of a soccer field surrounded by dense woods. The ground was covered with long grass and dotted with rock outcroppings covered with thick moss, blackberry and broom bushes, and an enormous oak tree near the centre. An oil-barrel incinerator stood on one side of the yard next to a mound of ashes with grass and old wood piled on top, ready to burn. I grabbed a sweatshirt and tiptoed past the door to the kitchen, where Martin and Mom were doing the dishes. I slipped down the stairs and out the front door, leaving it slightly ajar so they wouldn't hear me. A bright half moon shone in the blue sky even though it wasn't dark. I leaned against the trunk of the oak tree and massaged my arms. Even with my fleece I was cold.

I climbed onto a big rock, nestled my butt in a soft mossy spot, pulled my feet up, and wrapped my arms around my shins to stay warm. I rested my chin on my knees and looked back at the house. After a while I saw a thin line of blue light shining around the boarded-up basement window. I blinked and the window went black.

Thinking I must have fallen asleep for a moment, I stared at the window, eyes wide. After a few minutes a blue glow shone around the window again. My eyes watered and I had to blink again. The light disappeared as it had the first time. I pinched my hand – you know, the sleep test – and sure enough it hurt. So maybe I needed a test for crazy. I saw a light. I really did.

It was getting dark, and each time I closed and reopened my eyes the blue light appeared brighter than the last time. I shivered and stared at the house. Then, in spite of my damp bum and chattering teeth, I drifted into an uneasy sleep, long enough to dream a mumbo-jumbo of lights and scuffing sounds and thoughts that hung out around the edges of my memory. When I woke up, all that was left of my dream was my warm feet. The rest of me was cold and stiff. My legs hurt so bad I could barely stand up.

The house was black. The moon had circled the house and was casting long eerie shadows over the trees and lighting up the basement door. It was dead quiet when I staggered toward the house, and instead of heading around the front I went directly to the basement. It had never occurred to me to go down there – no one did. And it felt like I was trespassing. Just open the door, I said to myself. Like a thief, I thought, then, Don't be stupid. The door handle was rusty, and anyway, my arm wouldn't reach for it. It didn't matter what my mind said, my hand was not going to grab the knob. So I stood there for a few seconds, getting completely creeped out, and then made a dash around the house for the front door.

When I got to bed I found that for once I couldn't sleep. I lay on the bed, my eyes bugged open and my heart beating like a trapped mouse's. What I needed was a therapist, there was no doubt about it. I needed someone to talk to, someone who specialized in head cases. I needed to get a grip on my brain. My life was distorted into a shape I didn't recognize, like I was being morphed by some weird computer program – pull it this way, push it that way, and you end up with a long neck, bug eyes, and hardly a body at all. On top of everything else that made me crazy, now there was something bizarre going on in the room downstairs, and I didn't want to be the person to find out what.

Or maybe there was an easy explanation, and for that I didn't need a test: I was going nuts.

Chapter 4

For the next several weeks, Rose and I kept our distance. We sat side by side on the bus, but we only talked about incidental things like school and teachers and her soccer games. We were politely cool. Her invitations to meet her after school and my excuses that I had to do homework or chores were civil formalities. I wanted to back into a cave and cover the opening with a rock and disappear. I figured Rose would think it would be just as well if I disappeared. Who needs a stop-start friend that you don't understand and nobody else likes?

At Martin's place I developed a two-pronged survival strategy. Sooner or later, I figured, me and Mom would be out of there. For a couple of months – or at least until they got married – Martin had been good for Mom. She got up in the morning and showered before I left for school. She ditched her baggy T-shirts and sweatpants and pulled out her old sweaters and jeans. She had to struggle to get them buttoned in front, and they were a little tight in the butt, but they were on. She tied her hair back and put on makeup – a little too much blue eyeshadow, but, all in all, you couldn't deny she looked better than she had for years. The main thing about those first couple of months was that Mom smiled and even laughed. Smiling and laughing weren't something she had done a lot of before she met Martin. But ever since we'd moved onto the reserve, there had been a noticeable shift in Mom's behaviour.

She was on a downward slide – straight back to the sofa, TV, pop, and cigarettes. And surely Martin would get tired of the sit-on-the-sofa, baggy old Mom. It was only a matter of time, I thought – though it was taking a lot longer than I'd hoped.

Until the inevitable happened, I needed ways to occupy myself so I wouldn't lose what I had left of my mind. That was one part of my survival strategy. I did busy things like washing the dishes, doing homework, vacuuming the floors, the furniture, the car, anything. I cleaned my room every day in a desperate attempt to normalize my life. I rearranged the furniture in my bedroom until I had exhausted every possible place the bed and dresser and TV could be. Martin hooked up a VCR in my bedroom and I played movies day and night. It was a case of blocking out my bleak existence with Adam Sandler, Jennifer Aniston, Nicholas Cage, even Clint Eastwood – anything, anybody was better than the boring, dead quiet I hated so much or the creepy sounds I could hear in the basement.

Second, I turned off my brain. Forget the blue lights, the hot floors, and the sounds I couldn't explain. Forget the people, of any colour. What did they matter to me? I sure didn't fit in with the Indian kids. Yet blonde and pale-skinned as I was, I still didn't fit in with the white kids. Once in a while I talked to a girl in my English class. She was okay, but the only reason we talked was because during the first week we were put in the same group and had to work on an assignment together. A few kids from my other classes said stuff like "Hey, what's up?" or "How's it going?" I'd say "Nothing much" or "Fine." Otherwise, they all ignored me and I ignored them.

I may as well have been green. A glowing, radioactive green, I think now, because I must have been giving off some kind of a glow that kept everyone away. But I didn't know that then.

I thought it was everyone else's fault I was an outcast, doomed to life without a friend. So I thought, To hell with it, I'll just stop caring. Which, of course, was easier said than done.

In spite of how bad it got around there for me, Luke remained my lifeline. He could have been purple or orange or pink, for that matter, and I could have been any colour in the spectrum, it wouldn't have made any difference to him. He was a human being and that's how he treated me – like a human being. He was the first person in my life who put me on to the idea of being a human being first and all the other stuff later, like white or girl or Canadian or fat or skinny. It wasn't just me who felt that way around him. I doubt they would say it like I did, but everyone got the same feeling around him – he was important and you were important.

Luke was the kind of guy that other guys sidled up to. They cuffed his shoulder and said, "Hey, man, what's up?" Girls giggled, played with their hair, and laughed louder than usual when he was around. Luke was an all-star, no doubt about it. He looked like an all-star and everyone treated him like an all-star. And judging from the soccer, lacrosse, basketball, and canoe-racing trophies that cluttered every flat space in the house, even the top of the fridge and the back of the toilet, he probably really was an all-star. Luke looked people directly in the eye when he talked to them, letting them know that he was totally comfortable living in his own skin.

I think that was the thing people liked about him. It was what I liked about him. And I wished a little of it would rub off on me. If I'd had a little of Luke's confidence and cool, I might not have been so invisible and, at the same time, such a target for everyone to look at. Yet great as Luke was to me, he never noticed how I was feeling. No one did. In fact, if it hadn't been for Martin's mom and a particular lineup of circum-

stances, who knows? I might have become the invisible white girl who disappeared on the reserve and no one ever saw again.

It was the Friday after Thanksgiving. Martin was in his usual position, hunched over his bowl of oatmeal. But that morning he was wearing freshly washed black jeans and a new white T-shirt. His hair was pulled back in a braid and tied with a piece of leather.

I sat down and poured a glass of milk.

"Josie," said Martin. It was the first time I had ever heard him say my name and it jumped out at me like a foreign language. "Aren't you going to eat?"

"I'm not hungry," I said.

He stayed bent over his mush and didn't say another word until he lifted his bowl and slurped the last drops into his mouth.

"You don't eat enough," he said, wiping his lips with the back of his hand.

"I'm fine."

He was right. I hadn't eaten much of anything for weeks. I wasn't hungry, and when I did get food in my mouth I chewed it around a thousand times and couldn't swallow it. About the only thing I could get in my stomach was milk. I slurped and waited. Martin sat in sweaty silence like a runner waiting for the gun to go off.

Finally he said, "It's your mother. It's my mother."

I could tell Martin had started to say something important, but so far it didn't mean a thing to me.

"I'm in a fix," he said. "It's like the old people say, I'm between a rock and a hard place."

I had a notion to tell him that if he needed advice, I was

the wrong person to ask. I couldn't even figure out my own life. Hadn't he noticed what a mess I was? But the fact that he asked me felt good, so I paid attention.

"It's Mom's birthday today," he said. "She's eighty-eight."

"Holy."

No one had said a word about Martin's mom since the day Rose took me on the tour. The only thing I knew was she was in the hospital – had a broken hip or something – and Martin hoped she would be getting out soon. I'd seen her once, in the summer, whether before she broke her hip or after, I didn't know. She was a big lumpy woman whose soft body appeared to have been poured into her wheelchair like a thick milkshake. Her ankles spilled over the leather slippers she wore on her wide flat feet. Her cheeks were folded in layers with wrinkles on top of wrinkles. She had steely white hair cut short and curled. Soft pink lipstick covered her thin lips and a little more, to make her mouth look full. The thing you couldn't forget about her was her fingernails. Each one was long and narrow and painted a slightly different shade of pink. On her pinky nails she had painted red roses. She was the first really old person I had ever met and, big and crippled as she was, she was beautiful. I liked her instantly and was disappointed when they took her back to the hospital. She liked me too. She called me Granddaughter – I liked the way that sounded – and told me to call her Grandma, although up until then I think I called her Martin's mom.

"She wants us to come down to the hospital and have birthday cake. She ordered it herself."

"Yeah? When are you going?"

I asked so that I could pre-empt an invitation with an excuse to stay home. Yet in a way I wanted to go see her. I liked the way her voice, low and smooth and soupy, hung in the air and seeped into the corners of the room. When she spoke you didn't just hear her words; you absorbed them into your skin like body lotion. I could feel her as much as hear and see her no matter how far away I stood. But the thought of going into a smelly hospital to eat birthday cake made me want to retch.

"After supper some time."

"Uh, I don't feel so good this morning," I said, the weasel in me taking a quick way out. "I think I'll just stay home."

The disappointed look on Martin's face surprised me. What difference would I make at the hospital?

"You sure?" Martin said. "Grandma's pretty lonely at the hospital. And she said, 'Make sure my little blonde granddaughter comes,'" he added after a long pause.

I had been on the verge of saying, "If she's so lonely, why don't you go see her more often?" But Martin's last comment stopped me.

Now his face became more serious. "I hate leaving her in that place. The doctor said we can't bring her home until we have the place ready and there's someone here to care for her. Round the clock."

Martin had an expectant look on his face now, as if I was supposed to say something important. Yeah, sure, Martin – I'm going to know what you should do about your family problems. What did I know about families? Mine was almost non-existent. Anyway, I wasn't used to being in on this kind of adult-kid discussion. I was ready to bolt off the chair and back to my room at the first available opportunity.

Martin said, "What do you think?"

"What do I think about what?" I asked.

"Do you think she could move home?" Martin said. He

stopped, looked me in the eye, and then said, "I mean here, with the four of us."

A light went on in my head. The old house wasn't Martin's place at all – it belonged to his mom. And while she was in the hospital, Martin had got married and Mom and I moved in. No kidding he had got himself between a rock and a hard place.

"What about your mother?" His question had no more of an answer to it than "What about that hockey game?" or "What about all the rain we've been getting?"

"What about my mother?" I said.

"I haven't told her Grandma's expecting to move home," Martin said.

Ah, I thought. There's your problem. Martin's instincts were right. Lenore Jessop wasn't the kind of woman to look after old people. She didn't make tea and sit and chat. She'd never help an old woman to the toilet or scrub her back in the bath. Mom would never choose to live with a man and his mother – I didn't need to ask her to know that, and neither did Martin.

"Mom'll be fine with it," I said.

Which of course was a humongous lie. But Martin jumped at it gratefully.

"Do you think so?" he said, his eyes lighting up. Then his face flattened. "You don't really think that, do you?"

No, I think the whole idea sucks, I thought. I couldn't say that, so I said, "It wouldn't be easy for her, but what choice does she have?"

That statement was completely unhelpful, but it was completely true. Maybe it was something Martin should have thought of a few months ago, like maybe before me and Mom moved in. The look on Martin's face told me he was no longer thinking about Mom; he was thinking about how few choices *he* had.

"You should have told her a long time ago," I said – again unhelpfully. "At least she would have known what she was getting into."

Martin pressed his palms on his forehead, trying to force his brain to sort out the problem. "We'll move Luke downstairs," he said, as if he was just thinking but the words came out loud. "We can fix up a room for him down there."

"Where the windows are boarded up?" I asked.

Martin shot a disturbed look my way and then stood up abruptly, as if he had somewhere to go. He dropped his bowl in the sink, left the room massaging his coffee cup with both hands, and sat at his carving table, staring at his tools.

"Hey, Blondie," he said when I passed him heading to my bedroom. "Thanks for your help."

"No problem," I said, thinking, Lots of help I was.

"Don't forget about tonight," Martin added.

"Yeah."

I got to the bus shelter before Luke that morning. When he arrived, I shoved over to give him room to sit down.

"You going to visit Grandma tonight?" I asked. I was beginning to get over the idea of the smelly hospital and was looking forward to visiting the old woman. At least it would get me out of the house, and saying "Grandma" sounded good.

"It's Friday," he said.

"So?"

He gave me a look. "So I got places to go tonight."

I forgot, Luke had a life. Make that, everyone had a life but me.

"Where are you going?"

"Out with Troy and Denver. Probably to the pool hall in town."

"But it's her birthday. She even bought herself a cake."

"Really? Dad tell you that?"

"Yeah."

"He never told me. He just said I better get my butt to town with him tonight."

"I only met her once, but she's pretty cool."

"Maybe I'll catch a ride to the hospital and meet up with the guys from there."

It was quiet in the shelter. I listened to Luke breathing, and out of the corner of my eye I watched his body rise and fall with every breath. He didn't feel like my brother exactly, but then how would I know what a brother felt like? He didn't feel like a regular guy, either; there was no more reaching out and wanting to touch him. Thank God that little bit of insanity was over. That morning he felt comfortable, or I felt comfortable around him. I got a feeling that Luke and I were two regular people just living side by side, one day at a time. A plain and ordinary feeling that was totally new to me.

"You want to stay in town with us?" he asked. "You like playing pool?"

"Thanks," I said. "Yeah, I like pool, but I don't have any money. And Mom wouldn't let me out with you guys. Not in a million years."

"Just ask. See what she says. You never know, she might say yes."

Not likely. Luke didn't know Mom's history of no. In a way it didn't matter. It was nice to be asked, but I didn't want to tag along acting like a moron in front of Luke's friends.

On the bus, everyone got talking about the same thing – Bent Feather, the band that was playing at the youth centre that night.

"You got to be there," said Rose as she plunked herself beside me. She meant it. I could tell from the look on her face.

"I'm going to see Luke's grandma tonight. She's in the hospital. It's her birthday." I said it to her as if visiting the hospital was a big Friday night activity. It didn't matter – I had something to do.

"Oh, no way." Rose slapped her knees. "You have to come out with me tonight. Bent Feather's supposed to be a great band."

It was a leap over the gap that had been widening for the past few weeks. What was with her?

"I'll ask," I said uncertainly. "But. . . "

"No buts." Her voice had that I'm-not-taking-no-for-an-answer tone to it.

"I'll see. I don't know what time we'll get back. "

"Just come up whenever you can. I'll be there."

I knew if I asked Mom she would immediately say no. If I just went, I would have to walk all the way there and home and then sneak back in as well. The thought of walking through the woods alone once, let alone twice, freaked me right out. Sneaking out on the reserve was a whole different thing than it had been in town. I didn't even want to think about it.

At six thirty Martin and I were in the car waiting for Mom and Luke. I was thinking of Grandma in a hospital room, all alone, nurses coming and going once in a while. I wondered how long she had been there and whether she had lived with Martin before that. Was it Martin and Luke and Grandma before we came? Was it really her house? Were we keeping her from moving home?

When the others came, Martin turned the car around in the driveway so we were facing the road. He turned up the country music on the radio and kicked the gas. The engine of the old Chevy squealed as we shot off down the road. Martin didn't turn to look at Mom sitting with a stiff back, staring straight ahead with a sour look on her face.

"You staying in town with us?" Luke asked.

"No, I don't think so," I said, trying to be quiet so Mom wouldn't hear. "I'm going to go to the youth centre after. Rose is going to be there. And the band Bent Feather."

"Oh, yeah, big party tonight," he said. "We might see you there later."

"If Mom lets me out, that is," I said, motioning him to shush up. But from the look of Mom's mood I knew I wasn't going to be asking her anything. Something told me I was staying in later, unless I got a giant surge of courage.

The old car rumbled its way down the highway. The exhaust system sounded like it was attached with bungee cords to the bottom of the car. Fumes seeped into the back seat, so by the time we reached the hospital my head was screaming and I wanted to puke. Mom was fidgeting with her purse, Martin was humming "Thank God I'm a country boy," and Luke was fast asleep. One big happy family.

"What did you get your mom for her birthday?" I asked Martin as we fumbled our way out of the car.

"A present? I never thought of a present," Martin said.

"God, Dad," Luke said. "It's her birthday party and you never got her anything?"

"Did you get her something?"

"No, she's your mom."

Mom stood outside the hospital gift shop, shifting her weight from one foot to the other impatiently. Martin hadn't told her about his mom moving home, but she knew enough to think Grandma was a complication, and she didn't like complications.

I helped Martin pick out a bouquet of carnations and a tiny card covered in red roses. I borrowed a pen and signed my name. One by one the others added their names. At the last minute Martin picked up a helium balloon with *Congratulations* splattered across a baby buggy. Intended for a new mother, no doubt, but I could see that turning eighty-eight deserved congratulations.

You should have seen our grumpy, tired, poor excuse for a family traipsing through the hospital corridors and up the elevator.

"Happy birthday, Grandma," Martin said. Pretty soon the rest of us were saying our happy birthdays.

She was sitting with her back to the door, looking out on the hospital parking lot. She turned one wheel of her chair and swivelled until she was half facing us.

"Oh," she said in a tone that sounded like she had never expected us to arrive. "I've had too many birthdays for all that excitement."

The place was awful. It was no bigger than a jail cell. Grey walls, sick orange doors all scuffed up as if people spent their time in there running into things. My head had just began to clear from the stinky car only to plug up again with the thick body smell of the hospital. The whole thing was gross and I wished immediately that I had thought of some excuse to stay home. Once I was over the initial blast of the hospital, I hunched myself up on the bed. On the small metal table next to my leg was a foamy white cake decorated with bright sunflowers. Next to the cake was a knife, small plastic bowls, Christmas napkins, and plastic spoons.

"Put the flowers on the dresser, a nurse will take care of them," Grandma said before Martin had a chance to give them to her. "And the balloon," she pointed, "set it here. Now you sit down."

Martin pecked her on her cheek and stepped out of the way so Mom could greet her. When Mom bent down, Grandma wrapped her arms around Mom's shoulders.

"I hope you're taking good care of Martin," she said in her ear, but loud enough for us all to hear. Then she turned to Martin and said, "And you better be taking good care of Lenore." Grandma wasn't making a suggestion; she was making a demand. It didn't seem to matter to Grandma that Martin was pushing fifty. She was telling him what to do.

"And what about you, Grandson?" She turned to Luke. "You're not spending all your time with a soccer ball tied to the end of your toe, I hope."

"Happy birthday, Grandma. Don't you worry about me. I'm doing real fine. I might even graduate this year."

"He *might* graduate if he gets his butt out of bed in the morning," said Martin.

She laughed and turned to me.

"Come over here, young lady." She reached toward me. Her nails were painted green with sunflower appliqués. She cupped my hands in hers and rubbed them in a circular motion.

"How are you, my girl?"

Her hands were warm, and immediately I felt comfortable. If it hadn't been a birthday party with everyone there listening, I would have told her exactly how I was: going crazy.

"I'm fine," I said. "Thank you."

"Thank *you* for coming." She squeezed my hands. "It means a lot to an old lady like me when a beautiful young person comes for a birthday on a Friday night."

She patted my hands once more and then released them.

"I know young people have better things to do than to sit with me. But here," she said. "I have something for you."

Don't I wish I had something better to do, I thought.

She wheeled over to her bedside table, pulled open the drawer, and took out two smooth shiny rocks. She passed me a forest green, egg-shaped stone. She handed the other one to Luke. It was the colour of a tortoiseshell cat and flat as a sand dollar.

"A woman came around the hospital giving away these rocks. She said they calm you down and give you strength."

The stone was warm, and as soon as I rubbed it in my palm my arms felt like they were being massaged all the way up to my armpits. Grandma wheeled to the dresser and plugged in a kettle.

"You sit down next to Lenore," she said to Martin when he offered to help.

Mom was still looking a bit bug-eyed and confused. She didn't want to be there and she wasn't trying one bit to cover it up. She leaned against Martin's shoulder and watched Grandma line up four mugs, make the tea, and pass a cup to each of us. Mom tracked every move. It was as if Grandma was the first old woman she had ever visited, which, come to think about it, was probably true.

Martin and Grandma made small talk about carving and canoe races while she cut the cake and passed it around. Luke lay on the bed, putting in a smart-ass comment here or there. I rubbed my stone, spooned cake into my mouth, and watched Grandma move her wheelchair across the room and back, refilling our cups with tea and our plates with cake. She was in charge, moving from one to the other, conducting her party like a maestro. If she felt the tension in the room, she did a good job of ignoring it. She was having a birthday party and Mom's attitude wasn't going to spoil it.

As soon as we finished eating, Grandma said, "Now you don't have to be hanging around the hospital with me all night. You be on your way."

"Hey, Mom," Martin said. "We're here to visit."

"You've visited," she insisted. "These kids have things to do."

Martin and Luke and I got up and huddled around Grandma's wheelchair doing the hugging and thanking routine. Mom kept her distance, making sure Martin stood as a barrier between her and Grandma.

"Thanks for the cake," Mom said, popping her head around from behind Martin. She stood stiff as a board and arm's-length away so she didn't have to touch Grandma. Her lips were still so thin and tight the veins in her neck bulged like thick ropes. Her hands clamped on to Martin's sleeve, almost tugging his jacket off his shoulder as she pulled him toward the door. Mom was like a cat sensing danger – she didn't know what the danger was exactly, but she knew it had something to do with Grandma so she was going to keep her distance.

Grandma wheeled to Mom's side and stroked her

clenched fist. "It was good cake, don't you think?"

At Grandma's touch, Mom leapt backwards as if she had been struck by a jolt of electricity. Grandma held on to Mom's arm until she shifted her weight onto her own feet and relaxed her grip on Martin. After a long pause, Mom said, "Yeah," and nodded. "It was real good."

"You'll come back, won't you?" Grandma's face was huge with a warm smile.

Mom's lips fell open slightly and her neck veins softened a little. "Yeah, I'll come back," she said in an unconvincing voice.

Mom let go of Martin, walked out the door, and stood in the hall. Ignoring Luke and me waiting our turn to say goodbye, Grandma swivelled her chair until she was face to face with Martin.

"If you got a little space for me at home. . . " Although she didn't speak very loudly, we heard her. "The doctor said I have to get out of this hospital and into something for old people – or home if there's room."

"I'm working on it, Mom, really I am," Martin said. He forced his words through a whisper. His eyes flicked from Grandma to the door. Did he hope Mom could hear the conversation? Or not? Was he looking for the chickenshit way to tell her without having to tell her?

A wave of helplessness washed over Grandma, something I didn't expect from such an in-charge woman. She clasped her hands together on her lap and dipped her head until her chin rested on her chest. Her voice was so quiet I hardly heard her say, "If there's any other way, I'd rather not be put into one of those old people homes."

Martin's face had lost most of its colour. He looked overcome by his own feeling of powerlessness. I wanted to jump in and say it would be all right – Mom would be fine with it – anything.

Sensing the tension Luke piped up, "Hey, old grandma. We'll be back real soon." He messed her hair.

"You're as bad as your dad," she cried out and slapped his hand.

He grabbed the handles of her wheelchair, swung it around, and pushed her out into the hall. "Go, Granny, go," he called as he wheeled her down the hall.

I turned to follow, but Mom had returned and blocked the door. In a move completely unlike Mom, she stepped in front of Martin steeled for a confrontation, her back dead straight, her eyebrows curled in a deep V, and the veins in her neck popping out so far I was sure they were going to burst.

"You didn't tell me she *had* to move into your place." Mom shot the words at Martin like darts at the bull's eye. "I thought there were some options."

"*Our* place," Martin said. "She doesn't *have* to. And she won't – if you don't want her to."

"Ha, *our* place. Give me a break. I don't have a place," Mom said. "And now you're putting the whole damn thing onto me."

"No, I'm not." Martin reached out to touch her, but she recoiled like a snake ready to attack. "It's just I'm kind of in a spot, honey. And you're in a spot. And Mom's in a spot too."

There was strain on Martin's face but I think he was relieved Mom finally knew. He took the weasel way out and it worked. Mom knew and he hadn't had to tell her.

"And if I don't like the idea then I'm the bitch," she said. Her voice got shriller as her self-control ebbed away. She looked like a frozen branch ready to crack.

"Lenore," Martin pleaded, "you don't have to decide right now. It's her birthday."

"It's *her* birthday. It's *her* house. You're *her* son. You better take care of *her*," Mom screeched. I recognized the sound of her voice. It was the just-seconds-before-going-ballistic sound.

The tension had reached critical proportions. Neither Martin nor Mom was going to be able to avoid where the conversation was headed. The next words that were lined up in Mom's head (if she could say anything at all) had something to do with us packing our bags and heading back to town. There was no doubt about it. Martin knew it and I knew it. For a few seconds Mom was the only one who was not absolutely sure.

In those few seconds thoughts and sensations exploded like a string of Chinese firecrackers inside me. First, surprise – this wasn't how I expected it would happen. Then a flush of excitement – it was what I had wished for since we moved onto the reserve: we were going to get out of there. The excitement was immediately replaced by shots of pain that pierced my gut. And then a tight crawling feeling crept up the back of my throat. I knew that feeling – panic. The reason shocked me, but I knew it was true – I wanted to stay.

I had one of those near-death experiences. Well, it's not that I was near death, but my life flashed in front of me from start to finish and in perfect colour. The stench of the old apartment after the weekend; me and Mom alone; the parking lot behind the grocery store littered with pop cans, chip bags, and condoms; the arcade every night; Sarah and Katy and me sitting on the cement curb, holding our breath so we didn't pass out from the fumes while we waited for something to happen. It was grim and boring and I knew I couldn't go back there. It wasn't that I loved the reserve. What was there to like? But town looked different than it did before, and my life? Not good. In the next instant, like another film, the reserve rolled onto the screen And it didn't look all bad. Good things about it began to fly through my head. Walking to the bus with Luke. Sitting at the breakfast table with Martin. And Grandma – I had never had a Grandma who wanted me to visit her.

I began to rattle off the thoughts then, only semi-coherently. "I think it would be fun, Mom. We've never had a grandma. You or me. This is our chance. We've always wanted one. Remember?"

Mom looked at me with a shocked and confused expression on her face as if to say, Whose side are you on, anyway?

I ignored it. "I'll never get another chance at a grandma. Grandmas are good for kids. You said it yourself. That's the trouble with your mom. She doesn't know how to be a grandma." Oops, I thought, I better not get her going the wrong way. I said, "She'll be good for us. It'll be like we're a real family."

Mom and Martin gazed flat-faced with their mouths gaping as I babbled. If they had anything to say, their lips weren't moving. When Luke wheeled Grandma back into the room, Mom and Martin were leaning on each other like two rag dolls.

"We're going to go now, Grandma," Martin said. "I'll be talking to you in a few days."

Outside we opened the car doors without speaking and drove to the pool hall in silence. By the time we dropped Luke off, it was getting dark. The rest of the way home

Martin listened to music and Mom stared straight ahead. Info overload – she actually had to think about something, which she didn't do very often. I looked out the window at nothing, the events of the past hour churning through my head.

Was it true? Did I want to stay?

Chapter 5

Some days bring you more than 24 hours ahead in your life. It's like your back tires are stuck in the mud, spinning around and around, until suddenly you hit the rock and you take off. Life is like that. It spins over and over in the same place for days, weeks, even months, then something happens and you're blasted light-years away from the hole you had dug for yourself. That's how I felt. And by the time we got home, I knew the day wasn't over.

Looking like they'd had too much to drink, Martin and Mom staggered into their bedroom. They'd be asleep soon, for sure. I closed my bedroom door, turned on my light, and knew exactly what I was going to do. It was Friday night. If Mom was going to drag me back to the city, this was my first and last chance to go out on the reserve. I put on makeup, straightened my hair, changed my shirt, and stuck a movie in the VCR. Once Martin and Mom had used the bathroom their room was silent. I thought I'd wait ten more minutes, just to be sure. I lay on my back on my bed and closed my eyes, dozing. When the clock said 9:55 I grabbed my jacket, shut off the light, and tiptoed through the living room and out the front door. I left the door slightly open to avoid the clunk and creak.

I was pulsating with nervous excitement as I turned the corner and faced the road through the woods. For me, your basic wimp, this was a risk way out of my league. Waves of pre-winter chill floated across the street and straight through my jacket, raising goosebumps over my body. The night was sparkling clear, stars covered the sky, the crystal-blue moon stood almost directly overhead, casting a silver shadow over the tips of the trees and bushes and grasses that lined the road. If I wasn't freaking scared it would have been a beautiful night for a walk.

The only noise was the scuffle of my feet on the loose gravel and a dog barking from the farthest end of the reserve. As if in answer, another dog began barking. Pretty soon a chorus of yapping and howling mutts filled up the night like I was at a music concert. Once I was halfway down the road the woods crowded around me, thick and dark, keeping me faced straight ahead. No choice now – I was too terrified to turn around or even look over my shoulder. I reached in my pocket, expecting to find the green stone from Grandma. Shit. It wasn't there. If ever I needed calm and strength it was now.

My pace quickened, and I was almost running by the time the road opened up to the bay. The dogs had worn themselves out and all I could hear was the sound of the blood pumping through my veins.

The water was perfectly smooth and sparkled like a pool of black ink. Something told me to sit down, breathe deep, gather the courage, call it a night, and make a dash for home. Instead I found myself passing the beach and walking up the path through a field toward the sounds and light coming from the large stand of trees surrounding the youth centre.

At the end of the path I ended up in the parking lot at the side of the building. Panting from running or being scared, I wasn't sure which, I leaned back on my heels and looked the place over. Kids milled around the front door and music blasted from inside. Cars all crammed together with their stereos cranked clogged the parking lot. More cars lined the road on both sides as far as I could see. Suddenly I realized I was in full view of everyone – alone. What had I expected? That Rose would be waiting outside all night for me to show up?

I slunk back into the shadow of the centre and watched each person who passed the front door. I didn't recognize anyone. I didn't see anyone from the bus or from school. And I checked every face and hair colour. There wasn't one white girl – or white guy, for that matter.

Thinking I would check for Rose outside first, I inched my way up the side of the parking lot, carefully keeping myself camouflaged by the shadow of the bushes. Or so I thought.

"Hey, Blondie." A guy's voice came from a parked car.

I gulped a huge mouthful of air and choked it back, then swung my head in the opposite direction, away from the voice.

"Hey, you, Blondie. I'm friendly."

In spite of trying not to, I looked. Off to my right I saw a guy with his elbow resting out his car window. Shadows covered part of him, but what I could see beneath the bandanna on his head was long black hair hanging past his shoulders. Slivers of light lit up an eagle tattoo and crossbones that covered his forearm and elbow. He didn't look real. He was right out of a gangster movie – east-side, west-side stuff.

"Jump in." He leaned his head out the window. "I'm not dangerous." Other than the whites of his eyes and a glint on his teeth that matched his startlingly white T-shirt, he was very dark.

Suddenly another guy poked his head out the window from the back seat and said, "Hey, Blondie, there's lots of room here for you."

Frozen like a pillar of ice I said, "Uh-uh. No. Thanks."

"What's wrong? You waiting for someone?" From the slobbering sound of the voice of the guy in the back seat I could tell he was drunk. "You got someone better to do? Indians not good enough for you, Blondie?"

The driver revved the engine and the car lurched forward, trapping me against the bushes. The guy in the back seat leaned way out the window and tried to grab at my jacket. Fits of laughter blared from the car, but my heart thumped loud and the buzz in my head, like the roar of a vacuum cleaner, drowned out what they were saying.

"Hey, Blondie," said the guy behind the wheel. "Sorry. It's okay. Don't get so paranoid." The car backed away a little way, freeing me from the branches.

Suddenly a beer can came hurtling toward me. My reflexes sent my hand out and I caught it.

"Nice catch," the guy in the back seat shouted. I could see him when he moved out of the shadows. His face was huge and square like a bulldog's. "Now get in here and share it with me."

I dropped the can next to my foot. A scene passed before my mind's eye, like something out of a bad movie.

A young blonde girl hides in the bushes hoping the punks won't see her. She moves and they catch wind of her scent like dogs after a lame chicken. She runs. They run after her. She can hear them grunting and panting. They catch her and she tumbles onto the soft floor of the woods. They pile on top of her. She doesn't remember what happens next.

"You want a ride somewhere?" the driver said, snapping me out of my nightmare. I felt a thin line of something I could trust in his voice.

"No, no thanks," I stammered. "I'm going home."

"Let me give you a ride. Where you from?"

"The city," I said.

"Then you're a long way from home," he said.

"No. My home is right over there." I pointed vaguely in the direction of Martin's house although I wasn't sure which way it was exactly.

"Where's there?"

"Martin's. I live at Martin's house."

Then I snapped my mouth shut. I knew when the words left my lips that I should have kept them closed. Don't talk to strangers – the first rule for girls. And for God's sake don't tell them where you live.

I lifted my foot to step away from the car. The door opened and the guy in the back seat bolted toward me. Instinctively I dodged to one side and sent him stumbling into the bushes. My body and brain froze for an instant. Then I turned and took off toward the centre. Before I had time to think I was inside, edging my way through the crowd in the computer room and into the large room behind. For a second I felt safe, but then it was like a million pairs of eyes were staring my way. Frantically I looked around for Rose until I caught a glimpse of her on the other side of the floor near the band. She was talking and laughing and too far away – there were too many elbows and snarly faces between her and me. Suddenly I was struck from behind by a hip. I lurched forward and bumped into a big girl who was leaning against the wall.

"What the hell do you think you're doing here, Blondie?" The girl from behind yanked me back so I was looking her in the face. Christy.

I'd seen her before on the bus and in the halls at school. She never passed up a chance to throw me the middle finger or mumble something under her breath about me going home and getting off the reserve.

I gulped, and by the time I squeaked out a pathetic "I'm just leaving," she had turned around and was pushing her way back through the crowd.

As soon as I gathered myself up and got some muscle tension back in my legs, I made a beeline for the side door of the room and found myself on the path in the field. Outside I heard the drunk guy yell, "Zeb, where do you think Blondie went? Let's go get her."

I didn't slow down until I passed the beach and turned onto the street through the woods. Breathless, my lungs stinging from the cold night air, I walked quickly along the side of the road, staying close to the ditch. My body was in a high-alert, save-yourself mode. I was ready to leap into the cover of the dark woods if I heard the slightest sound or saw car lights coming.

My knees felt like puddles of muddy water when I arrived at the house. My bones vibrated from running and from the shock of being terrified. Just as I stepped on the front porch, a light appeared in the kitchen and I heard the fridge door open. I stood back and watched the kitchen light turn off and Martin's carving light come on.

I was stuck outside – no way to get in without being caught. Keeping my face toward the road, I stepped around the side of the house and through the field until I reached the mossy hollow on the rock. I settled my butt, pulled my knees up to my chest, and wrapped my arms around them to calm my panic. It was deadly quiet and eerie, but I was safe. I could see and hear anyone coming long before they would think to look out the back for me.

Eventually the thump in my chest and clashing sound in my head subsided. No one was coming after me. I leaned back and took in the huge night sky filled with stars. Gradually I heard sounds my panic had blocked out earlier. The cries of a flock of Canada geese, hundreds of them swooshing overhead on their way south. The eerie sounds of the night creatures, frogs, owls, hawks. Half awake, half asleep, I listened. It was music.

I woke up stiff and shivering, my eyes on the thin blue line around the basement window. Letters seemed to appear and fade on the window. I squinted to make them out. *No Trespassing.* They faded. I fully opened my eyes and the window was dark. I rubbed the goosebumps on my arms and legs, pulled myself up, and hobbled toward the house.

Luke was as startled as I was when I rounded the corner and faced him standing at the front door.

"Wow! What's up with you?" he said. "Where have you been?"

"Watching the stars," I said, sounding like every night of the week I went out at midnight and watched the stars. "I was bored."

It's amazing how half-truths and full lies spill out of your mouth so easily.

"Yeah, no kidding," Luke said. "The stars. Must have been fun."

Okay, so I'd have to come up with a fuller explanation

for Martin once I got in the house.

"You all right?" Luke said.

"Yeah, why?"

"You look thrashed."

"I'm okay." I was shivering so much I could hear my teeth chattering. "Just cold."

Instead of opening the door, Luke sat on the porch and motioned for me to sit next to him. I hunched down against the porch post and pulled my feet underneath me.

"I rule at pool," he laughed. "I kicked Tim's butt and Denver's and I made fifty bucks from some big biker shit that thought he could whup my tail."

He picked up a stick and burrowed patterns in the loose gravel. What was he doing? Why were we sitting on the porch freezing our butts off? Had he seen me at the youth centre? Did he know I was lying?

His silence made me uncomfortable. Silence was like hunger for me, waiting to be filled. Like the silences between Mom and me when I had been caught doing something wrong or when she was angry. Or when she was watching something on TV (which was most of the time) and I wasn't allowed to interrupt. Important conversations waited until she was in a good mood or during commercial breaks. I learned to keep my mouth shut when I wanted, so badly, to speak. Then I'd get to the point that my lips were so tightly sealed I couldn't open them even when I wanted to. No matter how much the silence was eating away at my stomach lining.

For Luke and Martin silence seemed to be something else. It was part of their conversations. Words and pauses formed a pattern that required the one as much as the other. Around Martin's place, silence didn't necessarily mean that someone was mad or that you were being shut out of their world. Silences were punctuation, like commas and periods and colons and question marks. Silence gave the words somewhere to hang. I was beginning to get used to it; just the same, that night I was worried that Luke might know something, that he might be mad at me or that I might have to explain myself. I wasn't looking forward to either one. I was guilty and I probably had it smeared all over my face.

"What were you doing out the back?" he said. He didn't stop drawing in the gravel.

"Watching the stars, like I said."

"Yeah? I haven't been out there since I was a kid."

"You should go out there. It's kind of weird, though." As soon as the words came out of my mouth I wished I hadn't said them.

"What do you mean, weird?"

"Well, it's not really weird," I said, trying to take it back.

"What, then?" Luke persisted.

"Well," I paused. My mind was racing to figure out what to say and wishing there was an eraser for words – the ones you speak – that could just rub them out.

Luke began stuffing grass in the holes he had dug in the driveway.

"Well," I repeated. "I was sitting out there and..." I paused again.

"Yeah." He looked up.

"I saw a light..." God, I sounded stupid.

"Wow." Luke laughed. "You saw the light. Where?"

"Shut up," I said. I was laughing self-consciously. "It sounds pretty stupid, I know." I laughed louder than usual, hoping to change the mood and maybe avoid having to explain myself.

Luke stopped laughing and said, "What do you mean you saw a light? Where? What kind of light?"

"Oh, it's nothing." I passed off the question as if it hardly required any thought whatsoever. "I was probably dreaming." I began to stand up. "I guess I'm not used to it around here."

Another silence. This time the silence was a challenge. It suspended the last words spoken up in the air, as if they were written on a billboard, and flashing underneath was a finger pointing at whose turn it was to speak. Another way Luke and Martin used silences in their conversations. And they were especially good at flashing that finger – your turn, your turn. I didn't want to, but I fell for it.

"Well. . . it's just that whenever I'm in the backyard, I fall asleep, or at least I think I do, and. . . " I hesitated, knowing I shouldn't finish, but knowing also that it was too late to get out of the conversation without saying more. "I dream stupid stuff that I think is real. Well, it's always the same thing, really – it's a light. And words."

There, I spoke, it was Luke's turn. I began inching my back up the porch post.

Luke ripped grass in long clumps and placed it over the deep holes. He was laying traps. Perfect. Someone was going to break their ankle.

"Huh, you're right. That's weird."

I think I could have ended the conversation there, but it was my turn, I knew it. So I said, "And sometimes when I'm in my room I can hear something shuffling directly under my bed. And when I stand up the floor is warm, even if it's cold outside. My ankles get hot and wobbly."

I put my hands over my mouth. That was enough. I slid back down the pole and closed my eyes. At that moment I wanted silence. But it was Luke's turn.

He stared at his land traps and said, "That's pretty weird, huh." He paused, but we both knew it was still his turn. "Woo-woo stuff. Dreams and visions and hearing things. A lot of people get into it. Indians do. White people do too, I guess. A lot of white people think Indians are all about woo-woo stuff. They think we're mystical weirdos that talk to the dead and listen to spirits and are related to animals."

Woo-woo stuff. I wanted to laugh. But Luke wasn't trying to be funny.

"I'm not into woo-woo stuff," he added. "I just stick to what I can see and hear. It's hard enough trying to figure that out."

"What if you see or hear stuff you don't understand?" I said. "Stuff that doesn't make sense in the real world?"

"I don't." Luke lifted his head, looked me in the eye, and said, "I make sure I don't." He tossed his stick on the driveway and stood up. "Just ignore it or it'll freak you out."

"What's with the room downstairs, anyway?" I said. "It's boarded up on both sides and no one ever goes down there. It seems like the basement is out of bounds."

"It is," Luke said. "Always has been as far as I know." That part of the conversation was over.

He placed his hand on my shoulder and said, "You'll be okay here. It's good for Dad to have your mom. And I'm glad it's not just me and Dad around here anymore. It got pretty heavy."

Luke opened the front door and let me in. Martin looked up from his carving.

"Your mom know you went out with Luke tonight?" was all he said.

"She didn't," Luke said. "She spent her Friday night sitting under the oak tree looking at the stars. I met her at the door a few minutes ago."

Martin continued to strip curls of yellow cedar onto the floor. He said, "Bored, are you?"

"Yeah," I said.

"Going to have to do something about that," he said.

"That'll be the day," I said. "Mom'll freak if I go anywhere."

"Going to have to do something about that, too."

For a girl who had had nothing to do just one day before, I was overwhelmed. A trip to the hospital, the possibility of moving back to the city, sneaking out, freaking out, and having a heart-to-heart with my stepbrother made a pretty full day, not to mention almost getting attacked by a bunch of drunk idiots. I lit a candle and dropped a CD into the stereo, then lay in bed and tried to unscramble the collage of images and thoughts that raced around in my head. One image rose to the surface of the confusion: Zeb – that must have been the driver's name – his black hair and the whites of his eyes and his teeth when he smiled.

I went over the event in the parking lot piece by piece, getting rid of the bad stuff, holding on to Zeb. He wasn't drunk. Or an idiot. And I loved his voice. I fell asleep to the sound of it saying, "You want a ride somewhere? Jump in."

Chapter 6

The thing that bugged me about people calling me Blondie was that I couldn't tell whether they were giving me a nickname or a backhanded insult. The tone of their voices made "Blondie" sound like a political comment, like when they said "white man" or "the government" or "Indian agent." One thing I got to know from Martin's conversations with his friends while I was locked up in the house during the summer was that they thought Indians had gotten a pretty rotten deal from every government since Canada became a country and even before. And though they never said so out loud, at least not when I was around, I didn't need to be a rocket scientist to know they lumped all white people into the same "government" bin. From there it wasn't much of a stretch to think that blondes weren't their favourite people. Maybe if I'd had dark hair and brown eyes it might have been different. I would still be a white girl, but at least I wouldn't be Blondie, sticking out there like a punching bag ready to take whatever crap people wanted to give me.

I figured out that there were three kinds of Indian people – well, at least Indian kids. I was totally invisible to the first kind. They walked past me, bumped into me, or stood beside me without giving me the slightest sign of recognition. To them, I wasn't human. I was another species or possibly an inanimate object like a door frame or a signpost.

To the second group I was neutral – there, but not important. If I happened to make eye contact or bump shoulders with these kids, they would mumble Hi or How's it going or Sorry. Luke's friends were in this group. Cory, his punk friend who had pierced every loose part of his face, was the friendliest. He talked to me in class and shared my textbook in math and my homework when he needed to. After school he'd slap me on the arm or say "What's up?" or "Hey, Blondie." It was brief, but better than nothing. At least it held out a slight chance that I could find a friend, but no one, not even Rose in the beginning, looked too interested.

Then there was the third group, which made a point of never ignoring me. It didn't matter how far away I stood or how invisible I tried to be, these kids would find a way to make eye contact. They'd shoulder in front of me to get my attention, then snap their eyes and turn away. When I was near, they'd grumble something under their breath, just loud enough for me to hear – stuff like "I thought this was the Indian bus" or "Why the hell is a white girl getting on our bus?" or "What's with the honky chick?" Just the fact that I was white seemed to be too much for them – like I was flashing a light in their eyes. They couldn't ignore me.

This group was made up mostly of girls. If I said Hi, they would blow short puffs of air out their noses, ready to charge and sneer. Christy was the worst one in this group, and Mary Ann, her friend. They were big and scary and never passed up a chance to give me a vicious comment or an angry snicker or the middle finger. Christy was the ringleader. She had the kind of face that looked like she woke up in a bad mood and went to bed in a bad mood. Her body, how she stood, and the way she stomped her feet flat on the floor when she walked gave you the impression she had a serious grudge against the world.

Mary Ann followed behind her looking half confused and half angry, as if she didn't know for sure what she was supposed to be mad at.

Up until the dance, Christy and Mary Ann made a point of confronting me every time they walked by, but they had never run into me or pushed me around openly before. At the dance it was a different story. And after that I tried extra hard to stay out of their way.

When you line people up in groups, there are always the people who don't fit into any group. Like Luke, who, like I described, will always be in a group all his own. And Rose. At first she was in the second group and then she confused me and I didn't know where to put her.

Saturday at lunch we sat around the table trying our best to act like a family. Mom wasn't saying anything – she was still deciding whether we were a family or whether she and I were heading back to town to make a stab at being a family on our own. Martin was concentrating on serving clam chowder.

"I hear there was a rumble at the dance last night," he said.

How did he know? What did he know? What was a "rumble"?

"Uh," I mumbled, wishing he hadn't brought up the dance at all, and hoping Mom wouldn't get into it. "I don't know."

After a short pause Luke entered the kitchen.

"Hey," Martin said. "Did you hear about the fight last night at the dance?"

"Yeah," Luke said. "Everyone's talking about it. I heard

that around midnight some idiots from the hills got all plastered up and started shooting their mouths off. Supposedly it was Zeb Prince and his gangsters. At least that's what they say. They piled on Lionel and Rufus and those guys. Lionel got ten stitches on his cheek and Rufus got a broken nose. Those jerks were using bottles. The rez cops got there and broke it up and a few of them ended up getting charged."

"Where was this?" Mom said. She had an antenna for trouble. She loved to talk about it. Especially trouble on the reserve and especially now, when she was looking for reasons to get out of there. "Was that right here on the reserve?"

"It was over in the village, Lenore," Martin said. "Don't worry about it."

"Who did you say the guys are?" I asked.

"Zeb Prince and his gang," Luke said. "You don't know them. You don't want to know them. Those hill country guys are always looking for trouble. They'd been hanging around in the parking lot looking for someone to pick on."

Instant chills sent goosebumps over my body, first fear, then something else. What had stopped them from choosing me? Zeb – he had stopped them, I was sure of it. I remembered the sound of his voice saying he wasn't dangerous. I knew he meant it.

"The village, Martin," Mom said. "It's just through the woods, isn't it? Are you saying there are gangsters around here?"

I tuned out their conversation. Martin could deal with Mom. I wanted to know about Zeb Prince. I wondered how I could ask Luke about him without giving away what happened. But Luke gulped his soup and was out the door. Mom stormed off to the bedroom – obviously Martin wasn't too successful in placating her. I hung around, helping with dishes and hoping Martin would say a little more. But he didn't say a word.

I had planned to head out to the mossy rock in the backyard that afternoon with a book and a blanket. Suddenly I had something to think about. I had a life, even if all I could do was dream about it. I dressed warmly and was just going out the door when the phone rang.

"Hey, Josie," Rose said. "I'm all dressed up with nowhere to go."

"Me too," I said, which wasn't exactly true. "What do you have in mind?"

"Let's do something, go somewhere."

"Come over," I said, thinking I had a better chance of getting a yes if Rose came to the house in person. Maybe if Mom met Rose again and saw that I had a friend, she might feel better about the reserve. "I'll ask Mom while you're here."

"I'm there," Rose said.

When I hung up the phone I got a rush of excitement. Maybe Rose would know Zeb. We could talk. Then I thought about the dance, and Rose, and me running home without talking to her. She wouldn't understand. I decided right then that I better keep my escapade at the youth centre to myself.

When Rose arrived, Mom was sitting in her usual position in front of the TV. Martin sat at his carving table whittling at a miniature canoe.

"Come on in," he hollered when he heard the rap on the door.

I pulled on my jacket and headed toward the door to meet Rose.

"Where are you going?" Mom pulled her eyes away from the TV for a few seconds.

"Out," I said when Rose appeared.

"I said *where* are you going?" Mom's eyes never left the TV.

"Down to the youth centre maybe, or over to Rose's house."

"No way you're going to that youth centre." Mom turned right around, her back to the TV. "It's not safe."

Rose screwed her nose up and squished a deep V in her forehead. Shit, not again. I remembered what had happened the last time Rose witnessed Mom in action. And from the mood Mom had been in lately, her attitude was likely going to be ten times as bad.

"What's not safe about it?" I said.

Mom's voice squeaked as if she had tightened her vocal cords. "After what happened Friday night? There was a riot over there. It's no place for a young girl. It's nothing but a hangout for roughnecks and gangsters."

"Mom!" I said in exasperation.

"Not a riot, Lenore," Martin said. "A rumble."

"Maybe a rumble to you, but it was a riot to me. That kid needed stitches, didn't he?" Mom lit a cigarette and sucked in a long drag. She curled her tongue and pumped out small rings of smoke into the air. "Martin," she said, "my daughter isn't hanging out at that place. It's crawling with gangsters. My mom was right. This is no place for Josie."

"Lenore," Martin said. He said her name deliberately with a slur of annoyance, which I hadn't ever heard from Martin, especially when it came to Mom. "This place is not *crawling* with gangsters. Josie is as safe as Rose. This is her home."

Mom looked surprised. The stern tone of Martin's voice had caught her off guard.

Rose swept in. "Don't worry about Josie, Mrs. Angus. I'll be there. I've lived here all my life and nothing's ever happened to me."

"That's not the point, Rose. *You* being there isn't going to help. *You're* used to this place. You're *part* of this place."

I cringed at the sound of Mom's voice. Rose and Martin exchanged looks that seemed to mean something like, We've heard all this before and didn't like it the first time. I thought, Here we go again. Mom's afraid and that always brings out the worst in her.

"Mom," I said loudly. I had to drown out her fears and the possibility of what she might say next. "I'll be okay."

She was cornered. She could see three against one weren't good odds for her so there was no point in striking back. She turned around and waved her hand toward the door as if she was shooing us out of the room. Loud and shrill she said, "Just go. Get out of here. But don't say I didn't warn you about this place."

"I'll take care of your mom," Martin said. He nodded to me and winked at Rose. "Have a good time."

I grabbed Rose's sleeve and dragged her outside before Mom had time to change her mind.

"Your mom's really got problems," Rose said. "*This place.* What does she think we are? *This place. Crawling with gangsters.* I guess we're a bunch of wild Indians?"

What could I do? I couldn't make the words go away. Even if I did have an eraser that could rub out the words, Mom's attitude would still be hanging out there like dirty laundry. The truth was, Mom *did* think everyone on the reserve was a wild Indian, except Martin. There was no getting around it.

"I guess that's what it sounds like," I said.

"I think it's more than just the way it sounds, Josie."

She walked three paces ahead of me toward the beach.

It was quiet – no cars or birds. Even the insects must have been hibernating. The only sound was our feet smooshing over the dead leaves that were soaked and flat on the road.

"God, your mom's just as bad as all those other stupid white people. I'm sick of them all," Rose snapped without turning her head. "Why did she come to live here if she was so prejudiced?"

Harsh. The words poked like icicles into my ribs. But Rose was right. Why did we come to live on the reserve if Mom thought Indians were so damn scary and if she was so damn prejudiced? I knew the answer. She fell in love with Martin – simple as that.

"Is Martin a wild Indian too? And Luke?" Rose was on a roll. "And me? Am I a wild Indian?"

My mind began to spin. My stomach tightened. Couldn't we just be friends? Did everything have to be so heavy and complicated?

"What about you?" Rose looked at me. God, she looked like she was going to bite my head off. "Is that what you think too? Do you think I'm a wild Indian?"

"No," I stammered. "No, that's not what I think."

"Yeah, I bet," she said. "Then how come you didn't come to the dance?"

I was stunned – a deer in headlights. If she wanted the truth, I'd been scared and, yeah, in fact I did meet some wild Indians, if you want to call them that. Who wouldn't have been scared?

"I did go." I thought I better tell her some of the truth, although I wasn't sure once I got started, where I would stop. "I snuck out and walked all the way there on my own. I even went in the centre, but that girl Christy started pushing me around so I ran home."

"Right," Rose snarled. "You know Christy. Everybody knows her. You didn't have to run home because of her. She's always got a bee up her butt. Why didn't you look for me? Were you afraid of all of us?"

"I'm shy," I said. "I thought I did pretty good sneaking out and running through the woods all by myself."

"And why don't you talk to anyone?" Rose asked. She wasn't going to just leave it with the dance. She had a whole lot more to say to me. "On the bus and at school. You never say anything. It's like you're too good for us."

Her steps quickened, leaving me two body lengths behind and looking for ways to defend myself. I don't talk to them? How about they don't talk to me?

"The only girl I see you talk to at school is that girl from your English class," Rose carried on. "That *white* girl."

"I'm not too good for you guys," I said with all the force I could muster. "It's hard for me, you know. It's not like everyone is crowding around wanting to talk to me."

Rose didn't reply.

"And I don't talk to that white girl all the time," I said, beginning to wonder why I had to explain myself. "She's the only girl I've met so far who's nice to me."

"Oh yeah," Rose said, almost shouting. "Well *I'm* nice to you. What about that?"

I was speechless. Why was I so much better at defending myself in my head than with my mouth?

When we reached the beach Rose leapt over the logs and finally slowed down when she reached the water. The tide was high and the water was lapping at her feet when I caught up to her.

"Sorry, Rose," I said, but I had the feeling my words weren't going to change her mind. I reached into my pocket and grabbed the stone from Grandma. "I'm sorry about my mom. And me, if you think I'm the same way."

The wind blew off the bay and bit through my jacket. I wrapped my arms around my chest and tried to control the shiver in my jaw. Rose plunked herself on a log with her back to the wind and hugged her arms around herself.

"Sit down," Rose said. She motioned with her chin to the log in front of her.

I sat down, knee to knee, facing her. By then my jaw was shaking so hard I could hear my teeth chatter. Rose watched me sit down. Her lips were perfectly steady when she said, "Don't say you're sorry."

I butted in. "No, but I'm –"

She didn't let me finish. "No, but, nothing. Don't say you're sorry for someone else. What your mom says isn't what you say."

"Mom's strange. She's not prejudiced. . . " I started to excuse Mom, but I knew it wasn't true and what I had heard earlier couldn't be excused. There was just no way of getting around her attitude.

"Don't make excuses for her," Rose said. She cleared her throat without taking her eyes off my face. "I get really pissed off when I hear white people saying stuff like that. I can fly off the handle 'cause I'm not like that. My family are not drunken Indians. Martin and Luke aren't wild and crazy. But people put us all in the same category."

I bit my lip and steadied my jaw. *I get it. I get what she's saying.* A light turned on in my head. I didn't know *how* she felt, but I knew *what* she felt, and that was enough.

"That must suck," I said.

"It sucks big time," she said. She gave me a fierce look, glanced away, and then added, "White people think they are so good, like they are so much better than everyone else. They suck, big time."

"White people?" I said. "You mean like me?" I did know how she felt – totally.

Rose balanced her elbows on her knees, cupped her hands, and sank her cheeks into her palms. She slowly shook her head.

"No," she said. "No. Sorry. I don't mean like you."

I was freezing. I yanked my hat over my ears and moved sideways until Rose's body blocked the wind.

"God, Josie." Her voice was muffled against her hands. "People are nuts. That's how I see it. You're nuts, I'm nuts, your Mom is *really* nuts. We're so damn hung up about ourselves we can't leave the other guy alone."

She thought for a moment and then said, "This is how I see it. The world is a mirror. When we look at other people, all we see is ourselves. Someone else may be standing right in our face, but we see ourselves, our problems, our stuff staring right back at us and then we put it all over them. Don't you wish it was a window instead of a mirror so we could look out there and see the other person instead of ourselves and our hang-ups?"

"Yeah." I wasn't just agreeing with Rose because her words sounded good. My head understood what she was saying, and right down in the pit of my stomach I knew what she meant. "Do you think it's possible? I mean, do you think we could really see other people the way they see themselves?"

"You mean without our big attitudes getting in the way?"

she said. Rose looked at me. Her eyes moved deliberately from my eyes to my mouth and my neck and then to my shoulders and hips and then my hands. She said, "I can't imagine what it must be like to be a skinny, blonde, blue-eyed, white girl."

I lifted my head and laughed.

"I know what you mean," I said. "I really know what you mean. I can't imagine what it must be like to be a dark-skinned, brown-eyed, black-haired Indian girl."

Rose's eyes shifted from my body to hers. Starting with her feet she looked at her knees and her arms. She craned her neck and looked up her arm to her shoulder. She raised her arms and examined the underside of her hands.

"Do you think the world looks different to a person who has different coloured eyes?" she said. "Do you think that looking out of brown eyes sends certain messages to the brain and looking out of blue eyes sends different messages to the brain? Maybe we see things completely differently."

"That's a crazy idea and I don't want it to be true," I said. I thought about it for a moment. "Well, if it is true. . . " I had a great idea but I couldn't find the words for it.

"If it is true," I repeated, feeling the words come, "then we should listen to how the other person feels and ask her what she sees before we assume we know."

"Yeah," she said. "That would be a change, wouldn't it? Anyway, what's the big hairy deal about being different? We're all different. Get over it."

"Yeah, world. Get over it!" I shouted the words into the wind. The sound stuck in the air with a thud, but I felt great inside. "And there doesn't have to be a great big ocean separating us," I said. "We can just accept there's different ways of looking at things – green ways, blue ways, brown ways, black ways, old ways, young ways, girl ways, boy ways – it goes on and on."

She was laughing when our conversation was interrupted by the sound of a car engine revving. Looking out of the corner of my eye I saw an old sixties or seventies car and recognized the orange flames over the front wheels. The engine cut and the door slammed and then Rose stretched so she could look around me and see who was coming.

"Hey, girls."

"Hey, what?" Rose hollered.

I barely breathed.

"Hey, girls," the guy said louder, as if he hadn't heard Rose.

She said, "What the hell are you doing here?"

"Can't you be friendly?" He stood directly behind me so I could only hear his voice, but I was sure it was him. My body froze, and not from the cold.

"Why should I be friendly with you?" Rose said.

"Who's your friend?"

"Josie?" Rose said. "She's none of your business, that's who she is."

"She looks cold."

"Weren't you charged with assault for smashing my cousins?" Rose said. "I heard you were in jail."

"You heard wrong."

He stepped sideways and entered my vision. His hair was in two braids like a Hollywood Indian. He wore a thick wool sweater covered with eagle and whale designs, baggy jeans, and hiking boots. He didn't look anything like a gangster. Maybe a hippie, and definitely cool.

"The assholes that were with me are in jail – they jumped your cousins. I drove away," he said.

I swallowed hard to keep my stomach from coming up my throat. I tried to turn my head, but my neck muscles were paralyzed.

"Tell your friend to wear a heavier jacket next time."

"What my friend wears is her business," Rose said. "Now you can leave us alone."

"Hey," he said, throwing his palms up. "I'm out of here."

He brushed his hand close to my shoulder when he turned to walk away. Jolts of electricity fired through my body as if I had been hit by lightning. Talk about sizzle. I didn't flinch, but every spark of energy in my body wanted to leap up and follow him.

"Rose," he called, "it wasn't me. You can even ask your cousin."

The car door slammed.

"What was that about?" Rose said. "What the hell is he doing here? He better not be looking for Lionel."

I shifted my butt on the log just in time to catch a clear view of his car as he pulled away. Maybe it wasn't Lionel he was looking for.

Chapter 7

Monday morning Luke and I rushed out the front door and arrived at the bus shelter just as the bus neared the stop. I stumbled up the stairs when the door whooshed open. Luke followed me and then shuffled past to the end of the aisle.

It was a good morning. I actually wanted to get on the bus. I looked forward to seeing Rose and talking, which was new for me. Now that we had crossed the ocean and actually connected with each other, I felt like I had a friend. The bus jerked and jolted and stopped what felt like every ten feet all through the reserve. I had walked five minutes to school in town, and it seemed like no one walked even five steps to the bus on the reserve.

The bus was almost full when it pulled away from Christy's stop. She stood behind the driver for a few seconds, scanning the passengers. Then, like a hawk that spots its prey, she stormed towards me. She was massive. She filled the aisle, her arms and shoulders hunched forward slightly, her chin and wide neck out in front. She had hands the size of Martin's. She wore stretchy tight pants that clung to her muscled thighs and narrow hips. From the way she looked she could have been a logger or a caveman – and she made me feel like a twig.

She said, "What the hell were you doing on Friday?" or

something like that. I couldn't hear her exactly because of the way she mumbled through her lips. Then she said clearly, "You better get out of here, white girl, or we'll make sure you do."

I didn't miss a word of that.

Instantly I froze – no air flow, no blood flow – just a cold burning sensation across my skin, lifting the small hairs like on a cornered cat. Rose didn't miss it either. She tilted one shoulder toward Christy.

"Whatever, Christy," Rose said, trying to pass off her comment.

Christy said, "Tell your friend to stay away from the youth centre."

"My friend can go to the youth centre any time she wants," Rose said.

Christy said, "Fuck you, Rose. You better listen."

Instead of talking back, Rose cringed slightly and sank back in the seat. She had stepped in on my behalf, she was on my team. It should have given me courage to stand up for myself, but it didn't. Instead, Rose was backing down as well, and I had never seen her do that. My mouth was dry and my brain was dead. Instinctively I glanced over my shoulder for Luke.

Christy had me pinned in the corner of her eye. "This doesn't have anything to do with Luke," she said. "I'm warning you again, you fucking white girl. The reserve is no place for people like you."

"Come on, Christy. Lighten up," Rose stammered. She didn't want to retreat, but I could tell she was scared.

Christy threw a nasty look at Rose just as Mary Ann pushed past Christy's legs and sat on the seat across the aisle from me.

"Yeah, you'd leave the white girl alone, cousin," Mary Ann said to Rose. Her voice was so loud heads began to turn, "if you knew what was good for you."

Christy shot an angry look Mary Ann's way and said, "Not so loud, stupid. You want the whole bus in on this?"

Mary Ann was Christy's sidekick but she didn't know the rules. Christy worked like a bulldog. Mary Ann was like a scrappy terrier, always shooting her mouth off.

This gave Rose a leg up in the conversation and an idea. She regrouped, stopped fidgeting with her purse, and held on to the back of the seat. She drew herself up so she was eye to eye with Christy. She'd taken a deep breath and shook off the glazed and confronted look she'd had a few minutes before. Rose was back on her game. Her eyes darted from Christy to Mary Ann.

"Forget it, Mary Ann," Rose said, loud enough to be heard at the back of the bus. "You don't scare me. *Cousin.*"

"She's with me, Rose. Don't forget it," Christy snapped, still in a half-whisper. "It's your little white friend that better be scared."

She stood up and sauntered to the back of the bus. Mary Ann brushed her purse over my shoulder and followed her.

I slumped into the seat. Sweat oozed out of every pore. Stinging salty tears were backing up against my eyelids. Running through the woods alone at night thinking a car full of drunks was chasing me was nothing compared to how scared I felt at that moment. Christy meant what she said, there was no doubt about it.

"Don't worry about her," Rose mumbled under her breath. "She's got something stuck right up her butt."

I swallowed a huge lump and coughed up the words, "For some stupid reason she thinks that me showing up at the dance is a good reason to take me on. I should have stayed home."

"No way," Rose said. "You don't have to stay home. She's just looking for something to bitch about. She likes to think she rules around here. She's always talking about who she's going to take out."

"Does she do it?" I asked, dreading that I probably already knew the answer.

"Yeah. Once in a while. But don't worry. She's not going to take you out."

The bus pulled into the school parking lot, and like a standing ovation, everyone stood up together.

"How are you so sure?"

"She just won't. We'll get Luke on your side. She'll back off," Rose said. "And if we need to we can get Denver and Tim and Lionel and some of my cousins. They all think she's completely nuts."

I hoped Rose was right. But I didn't like the idea of getting Luke involved. He probably already thought I was a pain. Half dazed I stepped into the aisle without looking. Mary Ann was in front and immediately Christy barged in behind me, leaving Rose standing next to the seat. Christy butted me with her stomach until I stumbled into Mary Ann. I grabbed the seat for balance only to have Christy stomach-butt me again. I scrambled down the aisle, flopping back and forth between the girls, until we reached the bus driver. Christy gave me one final push and I lost my footing and fell down the stairs. It felt like I had broken both my legs and maybe my back. But before I had time to gather myself up, I felt a hand grab my jacket and yank me to a wobbly standing position.

"Don't forget what I said." Christy's hand snapped back

and then released, shooting me forward staggering like a drunken fool.

Luckily by that time Rose had caught up and hooked her arm around my waist, keeping me upright as I stumbled toward the school.

"Don't be so stupid, Christy," Rose said. "You aren't going to get away with this."

Be quiet, Rose, I thought. Don't say it so loud. Everyone will hear. And please, don't challenge her. But Rose raised her voice even more. "Keep your hands off her. And don't finger me, you creep," she added in a holler when Christy and Mary Ann turned their backs to us. "I mean it." She hollered the last words at the top of her lungs.

"Don't worry about her," Rose said to me. "She's a mad cow. She throws her stuff all over the place. That girl needs therapy."

"Thanks" was all I could say.

I held my green stone between my fingers and stroked the smooth surface. My knees gradually straightened out and my lips stopped quivering, but I felt like someone had picked me up and shaken my body until all my joints were loose, including the ones that held my brain in place. For the rest of the day I snuck around the school, holding onto the stone, hoping to extract all the strength and calm it had to give me. At the same time I fully expected to be broadsided at any moment.

After school I found Rose and headed straight for the group of kids standing near the bus. There was already an expectant fever rushing through the crowd. I didn't hear anything in particular at first, but I could tell by the looks on everyone's faces that they had heard something of what went on in the morning. Even the diehard ignorers looked at me. At first Christy and Mary Ann stood off to the side, leaning against the oak tree, watching our every move. Slowly they moved in close enough for Christy to flick her cigarette butt and hit my pants leg. Rose grabbed my arm and pulled me through the crowd to keep kids between us and Christy. Within a few moments the two girls had moved closer and were standing behind us. We were playing cat and mouse. I was the mouse.

"You better get off the reserve, honky," Christy said in a vicious whisper.

"She can go anywhere she wants," Rose said out loud.

"Maybe." Christy cupped her hands over her mouth as if to direct the words to us. "But we'll be waiting for her."

Rose peered over the crowd. When she saw Luke and Lionel and Tim cruise up, she raised her voice louder.

"You'll be waiting for who?" she called out.

"Shut up, Rose, or I'll be waiting for you, too," Christy warned. "Keep your fucking voice down."

"And what are you going to do when you get us?" Rose ignored her warning and pitched her voice higher still.

Christy flipped Rose her middle finger and stepped backwards into Mary Ann.

Rose would have barged toward the girls if I hadn't tugged on her sleeve. "Come on," I said. "Let's get out of here."

"Up theirs too," she said. Her muscles tightened. "They aren't going to push us around."

"It's not you they want. It's me," I said. "They're your cousins. I don't want you to get into trouble because of me."

"Christy's not my cousin. And Mary Ann lets Christy lead her around like a stupid little mutt."

When the bus arrived, Rose pushed her way to the front of the line and pulled me behind her. Once the door opened we headed straight to the back of the bus and sat in the place reserved for Luke and the others in grade twelve. Rules aside – no one kicked us off. Christy and Mary Ann sat near the middle, facing each other with their feet in the aisle like bookends, shooting nasty looks our way until the bus pulled up to their stop.

Just as the girls stood up to walk off, Rose hollered across the rows of heads and over the voices, "Get off our backs, Christy. Leave us alone."

Christy swung around and mouthed, "Fuck you," and shot out the door.

What the hell was Rose thinking? She was pouring gasoline on the fire. Whatever Christy and Mary Ann had on their minds was now going to be ten times as bad.

"Rose, you're crazy," I said. "Why don't we just leave them alone? You're making it worse."

"No, I'm not," she said. The whites of her eyes were crystal blue, her pupils were huge and black. "I'm fucking mad. That's what I am."

It was the first time I had heard Rose swear. Although the word sat in the air a little out of place, it let me know she meant what she said. She swallowed and stretched her arms and legs as if she was warming up for a fight. "They're bullies," she said. "Everyone is so scared of them no one does anything." As the bus neared Rose's stop she picked up her purse and books. "They get away with anything," she continued, "and I'm fucking sick of it. They make us all look like racist imbeciles. Like we are so fucking scared of anyone who's a different colour that we have to run them out of the community. If their issues with being Indian mean they have to run down all the whites, that's their problem. They aren't going to do it when I'm around."

"I –" Before I had time to say another word she butted in.

"It's not about you, Josie," she announced. "It's about us. It's about people getting along with people, and I'm not going to let people like Christy decide who can be my friend."

It was the first time I thought it might not be all about me. Rose wanted to fight Christy for her own reasons. I was a little relieved in principle but no less terrified in reality.

"They aren't going to bully you, Josie. And let me tell you, they sure as hell are not going to bully me."

"Thanks. But how are you going to stop them?"

The bus lurched to a stop and a few kids stumbled down the aisle. Rose stood up and stood quietly for a moment.

"I'm doing it already," she said.

"How?"

"Everybody off that's getting off," the bus driver shouted.

"I have to go." She turned toward the door. "I'll phone you. We'll talk."

Luke and I were the only two left on the bus. He sprawled across the back seat and I sat two rows up, nervously wondering what Rose was doing to save my life from two wild animals promising to devour me at any minute. When the bus pulled up at the shelter, Luke dragged himself off the seat and followed me to the door.

A few steps into our walk home he asked, "You girls having a fight with the moose women?" His face was dead serious, but the sound of his voice made me think he was joking. I didn't think anything was funny at that point.

"Not a fight," I said. "We're not going to have a fight."

"You hope," he laughed.

Instantly my eyes filled with tears. How could he think it was something to laugh about? Christy could kill me with one punch.

"Hey, Josie." Luke turned and saw my face. "Those girls hate everyone. They're big and ugly and don't have any brains. They fight to make up for their mental deficit. Scrapping is their sporting event. Don't take it personally."

That was exactly what I was afraid of – that their threats weren't empty ones and it was going to be me this time. Just what wasn't personal about that?

"But they're really going to beat me up," I said. "Look at me. They could kill me in a second."

"They aren't going to beat you up," he said. "They aren't going to kill you. I'll take care of that."

When I got home I ran straight to the bathroom. When I finished, Luke was heading toward the stairs dressed for soccer. He paused when he saw me and stuck his hands down his shorts and positioned himself. Another thing I couldn't figure out about guys – they don't care who sees them. Would I be caught dead sticking my hands down my bra or down my pants, no matter how uncomfortable I was? God, there were things about Luke I just couldn't understand.

"Going to practice," he said, shaking his legs. "See you later. Tell them I won't be home for supper."

He threw on his sweatshirt and strode down the stairs two at a time. The door slammed and I was left a little dumbfounded, standing in the middle of the living room alone. The house was damp and clammy and felt like no one had been home all day.

For the first time since we moved in I had the place to myself. Mom and Martin were always home after school and on weekends. Supper was at 5:30 – you could set your watch by it – so I expected them home any minute. I walked into the kitchen and turned on the light before I grabbed a glass of milk from the fridge. It was only about 4:30 but the early winter dusk was beginning to cast shadows on the walls. I gulped down the milk, dropped my glass in the sink, and went through the house turning lights on. Not a good day to be home alone. If it weren't for Christy I would have enjoyed myself, but I had a slippery feeling that at any instant she was going to appear behind me out of nowhere.

I returned to the living room, flopped onto the sofa, and buried myself safely in the headrest and pillows. Looking straight ahead I caught my reflection in the black TV screen. My straggly hair hung limp over my shoulders, and all I could see were black sockets where my eyeballs must have been. I wore baggy rumpled jeans, a faded orange hoodie and beat-up running shoes. I was pitiful. No wonder Christy thought she could push me around. When I was in grade nine I wouldn't have been caught dead looking so pathetic. What had happened to me?

I glanced at my feet resting on the coffee table. Size 5. They would look like they belonged to a little kid next to Christy's feet, which looked like they were at least a size 10. A couple of kicks and she could break every bone in my body. Another look in the TV and I was disgusted. It might as well have been Mom slumped on the sofa, hiding behind the headrest, checking over her shoulder in case somebody was out to get her. It was an awful thought, but the longer I looked at myself, the clearer the image became. I was Mom exactly. Smaller, younger, but just as paranoid, curled around myself, sneaking looks around the room, expecting at any minute to be turned into hamburger.

I flicked on the TV. Oprah wiped my reflection off the screen just as the phone rang.

"Hey, Josie," Rose said. Her voice was right down to business. "I've got a plan. It's the only thing that will work. Last year a teacher told us what to do with bullies."

She explained that when you're bullied and you don't say anything, that means you're complicit, you're taking part, you're going along with it. Bullies gang up on you and pick and pick and threaten and threaten until you're so scared of them you won't tell anyone – and then they've got you. Who'll believe you after you've gone along with it for so long? That's when they've got you in the corner and you fold over into a lump and can't look up.

I knew that feeling.

"Bullies don't go away," said Rose. "When you're walking down the street and the bully is ten miles away, she might as well be right behind you because you're freaking out thinking she is."

I knew that feeling as well.

"Okay," Rose said. She was steady, like a military strategist. And as far as she was concerned her plan was foolproof. "The way to kill Christy's game plan is to expose her. We can't be afraid."

"Easy to say," I said. "But the truth is she's going to break our bones."

"Not if we get to her first," Rose said.

"No, Rose. You wouldn't have a chance against her. And me. . . " I didn't need to finish that sentence. "And besides, I got you into this. I don't want you getting hurt on my account."

"Yes I do. And this is not on your account," Rose said. "This is nothing new for Christy. You're just the latest person she has decided to hate. You're white. Easy target. It'll be someone else next week and someone else the week after that. You know Shelley, the girl with the blackberries?"

"Yeah."

"Last year I was walking home from the beach and I found her in the ditch, twisted in a ball, crying. I pulled her up like a baby into my arms and she had a gash across her forehead that was gushing blood. It took her weeks to tell us the story. Christy had put the boots to her and stolen her blackberry money."

There was silence on the phone. Terror shot through my gut. Christy was a monster. I tried to imagine why anyone would kick Shelley. She would probably hand you her blackberry money if you said please.

"No one stood up for Shelley," Rose said after a long pause. "Not even me. I was fucking furious, but I was scared and never did a thing about it."

I waited.

"The teacher said a silent community is a sick community," Rose said. "She said you have to tell people what's going on. Don't keep secrets or they will come back around your way and bite your butt. She's right. Look what happened. I didn't stand up for Shelley and now you're getting threatened. I'll get the same thing if I don't do something about it."

Rose's plan was simple. Tell everyone. She had already told her parents, cousins, and a few neighbours. She planned to tell kids and teachers at school. If Rose had her way, within a day or two everyone would know what Christy and Mary Ann were up to.

"You too," Rose said. "You have to tell Luke, Martin, your mom, and Grandma. Tell them everything."

"Won't the girls be furious when they hear?"

"So what? They're steaming mad already. We have to show them we're not afraid." She laughed. "Which we are, of course, but they don't need to know that. Second, we have to keep it right in front of everyone else – then it won't be a secret. And who knows? Maybe they'll feel stupid and back off. Like they did when we were waiting for the bus."

So that was what Rose meant on the bus when she said she had already started her plan. And it had worked. When she raised her voice and dragged me over to the guys, Christy and Mary Ann backed away. Temporarily. And that was the part that concerned me. They bounced back looking twice as mad.

"They are going to come after us like crazy women," I said.

"That's the risk," Rose said. "The thing is, Josie, we've got a pretty big fucking risk going on right now. We just have to turn it around and point it in the other direction. I'd rather it be in my hands than theirs. What do you think?"

"You know the girls better than I do," I said. I certainly hadn't come up with a better plan. All I could think to do was turn the lights on, hide on the sofa, and keep my eye over my shoulder and that wasn't going to do any good.

"No," I said with shaky confidence. "You're right. I'm just so afraid. And I hope it works. I can't imagine. . . "

"Can't imagine what?" Rose asked.

I paused to think of how I would work it out. "Can you imagine what Mom will do when she hears it?" I said.

"Trust me, Josie." Rose sounded in control. I liked that. "And let's not think about your mom right now. Well." She paused. "Maybe you're right. Forget telling your mom. But tell Martin and Luke. They'll tell people. Pretty soon everyone in this community will know what the girls are up to. It'll work. We're going to call them on their stuff, once and for all. It'll be like a circle will be drawn around them. They won't be able to get at their power. Their secrets."

Breathing whistled through the phone for a few moments, then Rose spoke again. "And besides, if they do kick the crap out of us, every finger on this reserve will point to them when it comes time to call the police."

"Let's not think of that part," I said.

"It's a plan, Josie," she said. "It's better than nothing and I'm sure it'll work."

After another long pause she said, "You'll need a strong mind."

The effect of Rose's plan – of there just being a plan – was amazing. I said goodbye and hung up the phone. Then I stood up, turned around, and looked. There was nothing behind me. Nothing to be afraid of. Immediately I thought about what I was going to do instead of what might be done to me. I'd have to make sure I didn't think too long and hard about Christy's boots or Shelley in the ditch, but I wasn't paralyzed.

I switched off the TV and looked at the walls and shelves and bookcases in the living room as if for the first time. The place was kind of fall-down ramshackle, and in all the clutter I had never noticed that it was like an eclectic art gallery. Carved masks, pictures, posters, and plaques hung in mass array on the walls. Things were framed in glass and wood or thumbtacked or pinned. When I say art gallery, I'm not saying anyone stood back and wondered where to place each piece. No one had asked if the pictures were evenly spaced or level. From the look of the wall, no one had said, Does this look good here or there? No, I'm talking about the kind of art gallery (if one exists) that takes each piece as it comes and just makes space for it. In fact, the wall looked a lot like the reserve when I went for the tour, a mishmash of things here and there.

There was one exception. Across the top of the wall behind the TV, Luke's school photos hung like a row of checkers, one for every year since he was missing his front teeth. The last picture in the row showed Luke with long hair pulled back in a ponytail, just like Martin. He looked like an artist. Now, with his hair cut short, he looked more like a jock. Either way – no doubt about it – Luke looked great.

Over Luke's pictures was another row of school pictures, starting with a chubby little girl and ending with the girl in a graduation gown and big eighties disco hair. She had a sombre-looking face even in the pictures where her mouth was smiling. The pictures were faded, yellowed, and curled at the edges – too old for them to be of Luke's sister. Anyway, I had never heard anyone talk about a girl in the family. In fact, no one talked much about any other family members, other than Arnie, who I assumed was Martin's older brother and not one he spent much time with.

The walls were loaded with sports pictures of Martin and Luke receiving trophies and ribbons, taking shots at the goal, pumping their muscles. There were old pictures of Martin, when he was a kid. Pictures of three kids, two boys and a baby girl, Martin always in the middle.

Near the centre of the wall hung a large picture of Grandma. She was standing alone in a field. She looked regal as the sun glinted off the line of her nose and the soft silver hair that tumbled around her ears. She was beautiful. When I looked at it, first I was hit by a wave of guilt, and then I got mad when I thought of her sitting in her stuffy hospital room, watching the parking lot, hoping day after day that we would arrive and bring her home. It was our fault she wasn't home already and I knew it. I started getting furious when I thought about Mom standing in the way, as far as I knew, doing nothing about it.

I stopped looking at Grandma. What good would it do? Then I glanced at a picture half hidden behind a lamp. It was taken at Mom and Martin's wedding; they were raising their glasses. I stepped closer to examine the shot. On one side of the picture was a leg, an arm, and half a face – cut right down the middle. It was me. Stepping in or stepping out.

I flopped onto the sofa, hungry and tired. I looked into the black TV screen and imagined the movie I was living. I got the feeling I had a supporting role, though I didn't know what it was, and I was getting the hang of being part of the cast. I dozed off looking into a black TV screen at the small white girl slumped on the sofa.

No Trespassing. The sign stood two stories high and flashed like a neon sign on the Las Vegas strip. I tried to turn and run, but hands out of nowhere grabbed me around my waist and pulled me toward the sign.

Enough, enough, enough. I bolted out of my dream saying, "You'll need a strong mind."

They were the words Rose had said on the phone. So what? Strong mind. I added up everything that had happened since Friday – Grandma, the dance, the parking lot, Luke and his woo-woo stuff, Rose, Christy. My mind had more than it knew what to do with. Chocked jam-full of junk was how it felt. Nowhere near strong. Maybe Christy was right. Maybe white girls should leave the reserve – with their white mothers. Then the Martins and Grandmas and Lukes could get on with their lives.

Rain and wind lashed at the window and the sky was black when Mom and Martin got home.

"Hey, Jo Jo." Mom was wearing jeans, boots, and a leather jacket Mavis had forgotten at our place the last time she visited. Her face was spattered with raindrops, her makeup slightly smudged, and her hair hung in strings over her shoulders, but there was a bright look on her face. She tossed a pizza box on the coffee table.

"Leftovers." She grabbed Martin's arm. "My honey took me out for supper."

"Thanks," I said. Right away I wanted to tell them about Christy and Mary Ann, like Rose had said. But the way Mom was gazing up into Martin's face made me think she might have gotten over her attitude about Grandma and leaving. Maybe we were staying and they'd solved the Grandma problem. I didn't want to wreck that. Timing was everything and I was starving, so I concentrated on eating instead.

Chapter 8

You would think that if there was ever a time I would have wanted to turn and run, it would have been then. First the guys at the youth centre and then Christy and Mary Ann. But strange as it may seem, it had the opposite effect. Fear had a way of straightening out my confusion. Things were better between Rose and me, and Luke was moving clearly into my brother role – just like the brothers in my little girl dreams. Even if I didn't get the answers I needed from him, he was there for me. So as scared as I was, it didn't make me think about moving back to the city. The only reason I would have wanted to move out was so Grandma could move home, but that seemed to be still up to Mom to decide.

Looking back at what was happening to me, I now realize that before I moved to the reserve I was squinting with blinders on my eyes. All I could see was a tiny stream of vision that was straight ahead – the easy stuff I wanted to see. A grocery-store daffodil stuffed in a plastic pot, foil wrapped. That was me. And the thing about it was, I liked it. Making sure I only saw what I wanted to see and did what I wanted to do – wrapped up in the mall, my friends, the arcade. And I liked it. I liked being safe in the centre of my little universe, part of the transparent people who didn't have to think about stuff much. Who wouldn't like that?

I'm not saying that the reserve or anyone in it consciously taught me anything. I just got transplanted, that's all. I got tipped out of the plastic pot and dumped in the field where the wind blows and it rains – forget the fancy foil. It didn't help that I was transplanted into a field of tulips or Easter lilies or whatever they were – I was the only daffodil anywhere. And once I was out there, plunked in the middle of nowhere, I had no choice but to open my eyes, and it freaked me out. I was so desperate to see something familiar. But when I was awake I didn't like anything I saw or heard. When I was asleep my dreams made no sense. Yet, either way, I couldn't close my eyes – I couldn't shut the stuff out. Too late for me. Nothing else I could do but get on with it.

After a while I caught on that maybe the real meaning of my life was there, but it was still just out of my vision. It wasn't centred on me, exactly. It was happening all around – bigger than me and slightly beyond my reach. To begin with, I hated the feeling. I wanted my pot back and the foil wrap. Field daffodils get too much sun; the light gets at you and the wind wears you down. Life was getting real, but that didn't mean it was easy. Like in the wedding picture, I was stepping into the scene.

When the alarm blared at 6:30 the next morning, I woke up with a jolt. My garbled dreams faded quickly, leaving me feeling like a space traveller who wakes up just in time to land – slightly out of sync but ready to meet the challenge. I knew what I had to do.

Martin was shuffling around in the kitchen and the smell of hot oatmeal wafted through the house. I tapped on Mom's bedroom door.

"Uumm?"

"Can I come in?"

"Uumm."

I opened the door slightly.

"Mom, are you awake?"

"Uh-uh."

She rolled over on her side, motioning for me to sit beside her. Her eyes were closed and she breathed sleepily.

"You okay, Mom?" I asked.

"Yeah," Mom said.

"You sure?"

"Yeah."

"You'd tell me if you weren't okay?"

Mom opened her eyes and looked at me suspiciously. Then she pulled herself up to a sitting position. "Would you tell me if *you* weren't okay?" she asked.

"I don't know," I said. "Probably."

Mom started to drift downward.

"Mom," I said to wake her up again. "Are we going to be staying around here? Or are we leaving?"

It was the most direct question I had asked Mom in a long time. She struggled to keep herself upright, grabbing my hand.

"Do you hate it here, Josie?" Mom asked, unusually clear-headedly.

"No," I said. "I don't."

I paused for a moment, not used to telling Mom much of anything. But it was different that morning. I got the feeling, even though she was hardly awake, that she wanted to know how I felt. And I wanted to tell her.

"I mean, I did want to leave," I said. "If you had asked me last week I would have said yes."

"Me too," she said. "This is a tough place."

"Yeah."

Then she looked at me thoughtfully and asked, "What changed for you, Jo Jo?"

"I don't know," I said, though I had a few ideas. "Maybe I've just gotten used to it."

"I don't think that I'll ever really get used to this place," Mom said with a shudder.

This place. Nothing had changed for her, it seemed. I wanted to spout off something to her about her attitude but decided against it. We were on the same side, even if it was only for a few moments, and even if it was just because she was half asleep. I didn't want to spoil it.

"So are we staying around?" I said. Of course Mom hadn't said anything definitive.

"Yeah." Mom crawled back under the covers. "It's Martin, Jo Jo. I can't leave him."

I wanted to ask about Grandma but thought I'd better not push it. "Love you, Mom."

"Love you, Jo Jo."

I closed the door softly behind me.

"Morning," I said when I tipped the saucepan and scooped some mush in my bowl.

"Morning," Martin said. He pushed his chair back from the table. "Thank you for helping me out the other night," he said.

I looked at him and frowned. Helping him out with what?

"At the hospital, with Mom and Lenore," Martin said.

"Oh, yeah," I said. "Is everything going to be okay?"

"I think so," he said. "I left it alone and now Lenore's got a great idea. She figures Mom should move in here." Martin smirked. "Lenore says it would get Mom out of the hospital and you'd have the grandma you've always wanted."

He dropped his jaw in mock amazement. "A great idea, don't you think?"

"Yeah, good for her," I said, pretty disgusted that Mom was so dumb and Martin knew it. "When's it going to happen?"

He chuckled and said, "Give your mom a little more time and she'll decide when it's all going to happen." Then he dipped his head and winked. "It'll happen when the time is right, Josie. No point hurrying it up or it'll just push itself up in front of our face, get in our way, and slow us down again. Mom knows that." He scraped the bottom of his cereal bowl.

Was Grandma really okay with waiting around until Mom was ready? I wasn't sure Martin or Grandma had any idea how long that could be.

But Martin seemed willing to wait. That was the way he was – easy come, easy go. His voice was slow and methodical, like he had all the time in the world. His movements appeared deliberate, as if the speed on the screen was slowed half a pace. There was never a rush with Martin.

On the other hand, he was a conundrum. If time didn't matter how come you could set your watch by the time he got up, made breakfast, and cooked supper? If life was so easy come, easy go, why were the glasses in such perfect rows in the cupboard? And the fridge, why was it organized like a filing cabinet? Each thing had an exact place – milk in the middle, cheese next to it, juice to the left side. If you tossed the milk carton to one side or the other, Martin would open the fridge and place it back in its right spot. And you should have seen the cutlery drawer. It was divided with wooden partitions and lined with terry towel. Each knife was set out with the blade facing the same direction, each fork exactly lined up with the one beside. And the pot cupboard – I'll just say that it would not have been out of place in an army kitchen. Yet I never saw Martin get upset or raise his voice. And with Mom? He was ten times as patient as I would have been.

"Morning."

"Morning."

"Morning."

As usual Luke sat down at the last moment. It was almost time to catch the bus. I forgot about Martin and thought about Rose. I had to take care of business. As soon as she got on the bus, I knew she was going to ask me if I had told Luke and Martin about Christy and Mary Ann.

Before I had time to think any more about it I blurted out, "Christy and Mary Ann have threatened to beat me up. And now they're after Rose, too."

Luke still had his spoon in his hand but he stopped eating. "You really worried about that?" he said, frowning at me.

"Yeah," I said.

Martin was standing at the sink rinsing his bowl. "Christy?" He turned and looked at Luke for clarification. "Is she Vicky's daughter?"

"Yeah," Luke said. "The oldest one. There are a few of them." He continued eating and talking at the same time. Something I would have had a lot more trouble stomaching if I hadn't been so interested in what he had to say. "She's right out of control these days. Got one bad attitude that won't quit. Mary Ann's Rose's cousin. She wasn't so bad before she started hanging out with Christy. Together they're brutal."

"What do you mean?" Martin turned off the tap and leaned back against the sink.

"Christy's the one who put the boots to Shelley, the Jackson girl, and stole her money," Luke said. "Remember? She made a real mess of her."

"Vicky's had trouble with those kids since Monty disappeared. They're a bunch of wild Indians."

Martin said stuff like that without even a flicker of an apology. It was his way, he said, of exercising his freedom of expression. Martin said he was not going to be told what to say by Indians or by white people. One day I raised my eyebrows at the language he was using and he said, "Oh, they all try to shut us up, Josie. But I'm a free man. I see things my way. I call things my way. And I tell the story using whatever words I want. I haven't come all this way in life just to suck honey and say it was all a holiday."

Martin was stroking his chin. "They've always been a little crazed."

"Rose says I have to tell everyone. She said if we expose them they'll back down," I said. "What do you guys think about that?"

Martin and Luke both spoke at the same time. Martin said, "She's right." Luke said, "That'll just get them madder."

They stopped and examined each other like two drivers who had just collided.

"If we keep hiding our problems, they'll eat us up," Martin said. "Just look at this. Vicky used to beat girls up when I went to school. She beat my cousin so bad the girl was never the same after. Now her daughter's doing the same thing."

Luke slurped the milk out of his bowl and stood up. As he leaned against his chair, the frown dropped from his face and he said, "You're right. Why shut up about it? Just make sure you don't get stuck somewhere alone."

Their serious tone confirmed everything I had already thought. I was in big trouble and Rose's plan was no guarantee I wouldn't get hurt. Wonderful. I was hoping for something a little more comforting from Martin, at least.

As Luke and I left the kitchen, Martin said, "Don't back down from bullies, Josie. Us Indians did that for years. We got bullied by one damn government after the other and we never stood up for ourselves. It sure as hell never did us any good. We're only figuring that out now. So you learn the lesson, girl, and stand up to them. And Luke," he called, "you better watch out for the girls too. Tell your friends the same thing."

For the next few days, Christy and Mary Ann lurked around the halls like dark shadows. Wherever I was, they showed up. They leaned against the walls outside my classes shoulder to shoulder and waited at the washroom like doorposts. All indications pointed to the washroom as the likely location for a confrontation, so I developed a strategy: only take a pee if I absolutely couldn't hold it, wait until the washroom was crowded, pee as fast as I could, and never get left in there alone.

That was part of my overall strategy against Christy – instinctively defensive. I stuck close to Luke or Rose whenever I could. I lingered around classrooms where there were teachers and made sure I was part of a crowd wherever I went.

The offensive part – telling everyone – I wasn't so good at. I knew it was the right thing to do; I just couldn't seem to open my mouth. For one thing, in spite of Rose's plan, all I could think about was how to stay out of their way. A basic wimp is what I am saying. And for another thing, who was I going to tell? I didn't know anyone. I wasn't going to casually walk up to someone and say, "Hey, did you know those girls want to kill me?"

So it was mostly Rose who took the offensive. If she saw the girls looming near us she would wait until a few kids gathered or a teacher walked by and then holler "Keep your hands off us" or "What do you think you're doing?" She lined people up to watch out for me. That's how I got to know Ramona, a girl in my gym class, bigger than Christy and meaner looking, too. It made me feel like a bit of an idiot, but I was happy enough when Rose asked Ramona to hang out with me if Christy ever showed up in the change rooms. Christy never showed, but Ramona was pretty cool. She told me she used to hate white people like Christy did. She said she was still not crazy about a lot of them and the way they acted. But one day she realized she wasn't crazy about all the Indians and the way they acted either, so she laid off hating people altogether.

"You know, Josie," she said after class when she was standing in the change room stark naked. She was the only girl who showered after class, and she didn't cover up or change quickly and discreetly behind a towel. In fact, she was quite a sight – one girl stripped down, walking around the change room, while all the other girls hid behind towels and partitions for privacy. "I don't like a lot of things about this fucking life. But one thing I decided was that I wasn't going to hate everything about it either. Hating just eats your guts out. Once you're into hate there's no stopping it, and it creeps around like an assassin and takes out everything in its path."

Ramona surprised me the way she spoke. You could tell she'd been through some rough stuff, but she never mentioned it. She didn't live on the reserve and she moved away soon after she played my bodyguard, which was disappointing because she could have shown Christy a thing or two.

Other than Ramona, Rose's tactics scared the hell out of me. She made the girls so mad that steam was almost visible coming out of their nostrils when they walked down the hall. They were like two raging bulls being held back by a thin wire fence. It was only a matter of time before they were going to charge at us. I couldn't get my mind off Martin's cousin who wasn't quite right anymore and the scars on Shelley's face.

By Friday afternoon I was exhausted. Rose had been planning to carry on with the publicity campaign at the youth centre, but she took pity on me and declared instead that Saturday would be girls' day, at her house. "If you're going to lurk inside all day, you might as well have fun," she said.

We ate microwaved pizzas, popcorn, and pasta, talked about clothes and soccer and teachers and Christy and Mary Ann, and watched reality TV and talk shows.

"If your mom watches this crap all day it's no wonder she's so paranoid," Rose said when we were watching a talk show about rape, but that's as far as that topic went.

I found out that it wasn't the Luke connection after all that had made Rose want to be my friend.

"My cousin Lara," she said. "We'd been friends since we were born." Rose's eyes filled with tears and then she laughed. "I'm such a sap. I still can't talk about her."

She swallowed and told me that she and Lara were together every day until Lara's father ran off with Tim's mother. Lara and her mother moved up north to her mother's village. Rose had hardly heard from her since. "So," Rose said, "I needed a friend as much as you did."

She blew her nose and then right out of the blue she said, "That was Zeb, you know? That afternoon at the beach. The guy that put the stitches on Lionel."

I had an instant gut-and-heart-and-head scramble. Every nerve in my body sizzled like they were live wires rubbing against each other, and the word "Zeb" was the electrical current.

"I thought it was his friends that did that," I said. My mind dashed back to the sight of the drunken guy lunging out of the back of Zeb's car.

She said, "Yeah, that's what he said." Her forehead flattened. "Zeb sure was interested in you. Don't you think?"

Again, the jolt. When Rose said his name, it almost hurt. I had to be careful or I'd find myself spilling the whole story of what happened at the youth centre.

"Me?" I laughed in what I hoped was a convincingly doubtful way. "He was probably just bored."

"Yeah." Her voice sounded convinced. "He's staying with his aunt. She lives over on the other side." Her hand swung loosely in the direction of the youth centre.

"Does the reserve go out that direction?" I asked, seizing on a more neutral topic.

"Used to, before they put the highway through," she said. "There are still a few houses over that way on the other side of the new road."

But I wanted to talk about Zeb. I wanted to think about him. I'd been so paranoid about Christy I hadn't had time to think about anything else. The memory of Zeb's hand near my shoulder sent another current surging through my body, intercepting my caution. I blurted out, “He’s kind of cute, don’t you think?”

Rose gasped, “Uh, Josie! I think he’s sick.” She stuck her finger down her throat, feigning a gag. “That car, his tattoo, and those long braids – he’s straight out of the eighties. Or was it the seventies?”

“Hey,” I said, “I like the seventies look.”

Which was a lie. Up until then I thought the seventies were stupid.

“No way, Josie.” Rose laughed. “He’s way too weird. He’s a seventies, hippy, east-side, nineties gangster. Take your pick.”

We giggled – no accusations, no suspicion. We giggled like girls.

“I guess that’s it,” I said. “Gangster hippy. That’s my style.”

The subject of Zeb turned into boy talk and more boy talk. But I succeeded in avoiding any mention of the night at the youth centre. I don’t know why I didn’t just tell Rose, but once I had turned it into a secret I didn’t know how to change my story without her thinking I wasn’t being honest with her. And now that we were friends I didn’t want any more tension between us.

“Are you sure you’re okay to walk home alone?” Rose said. She handed me my hat and scarf. “I’ll walk with you if you want.”

“I’m fine,” I said. “I’m sure Christy and Mary Ann have better things to do than lurk in the woods all day waiting for me to show up.”

“You just watch out for gangsters and seventies guys. They love blonde hair,” Rose hollered as I ran down her driveway.

“Thanks, Rose,” I shouted back. “I’ll watch out all right.”

I sprinted down the reserve road to the beach. I was cold and excited and not quite as brave as I thought. I dashed through the woods hoping to avoid even the thought of Christy and Mary Ann lurking behind me. It was the thought of the black car pulling up behind me that put the shudder in my stomach.

Daydreams.

"Sure, thanks for the ride," I would say. I would climb into the passenger seat. He would lean over and close the door. I would turn my head. His face would be so close to mine I would feel his skin. I would breathe in and catch a whiff of his smell. "Just drop me off at the corner."

Cold air blasted against my face, but when I got home I was warm and tingling all over. That night I lay in bed, thinking about the day. A week that had started on the brink of disaster had ended with the best day of my life. Rose was my friend – the ocean between us was shrinking. I pulled my head into the blankets and closed my eyes.

A thin metallic sound floats through the night air. It's coming from behind the blue light. A cat is crying. A small thin cat is crying, Let me out! The sound gets louder and louder. The light pulses like a heartbeat. It's the Las Vegas sign again, fading in and out of the blue around the words NO TRESPASSING. The music playing. . . it's not music. It's crying. Thin, metallic crying. It's a tin cat.

I sat up and yanked the blanket away from my face. I looked at the clock. The numbers looked odd, like pickets on a fence: 11:11. The sound of crying was still ringing in my ears. I gathered the covers around me and dashed to Martin and Mom's room. I knocked, then went in.

"There's someone crying," I said.

Mom groaned. Martin sat up. "Crying? Who's crying?"

"I don't know," I said. "Maybe downstairs." I could still hear the eerie sound in the back of my head.

Martin tensed up. "I can't hear anything," he said.

I stood still. It was dead quiet.

"Neither can I," I said. "Not anymore."

"You dreaming?" he said.

"Yeah," I said. "It sounded pretty strange. I was sure someone was crying. Downstairs. And I've heard the sound before."

"No one is downstairs," Martin said sternly. "You must have been dreaming. Go back to bed."

Chapter 9

The bullying thing – it becomes your life. Nothing else is going on when you are looking over your shoulder wondering when or where the monster is going to show up. I went from no life at all – the nobody, the weird white girl who hung out with the Indians although they didn't want her to – to the white girl Christy was going to cremate. It wasn't a transition I would have chosen for myself, but it changed things in a way I would never have imagined.

Mostly it changed the other kids. Kids who had never so much as looked at me in the past began to say hi to me. Kids I had never seen before knew my name. I didn't need Rose's help to find company wherever I went; I had it, sometimes more than I wanted. And not just the Indian kids, either. Thanks to Rose's campaign, everyone knew what was going on.

If my life in those days had been a movie, the background music would have been the crescendo in a classical symphony: the kettle drum roll, the whine of the violins, the howling of the brass and woodwinds. The scene was rolling and there was no stopping it. We were all just waiting for that cymbal crash. . .

The girls – that's what they became known as, "the girls," sort of like calling them "the gang" or "the thugs," as if they belonged to a club or something – had two choices: back off because of group pressure or follow through with their threats even though everyone knew about it. I didn't think Christy was the kind of girl who would have made a plan. She seemed more the time bomb kind of girl: the pressure was building and she was going to explode, it was only a matter of time. But she was methodical and nothing fazed her, which in terms of mind games gave her the decided upper hand. When you expect someone to do the unexpected and then they don't, and then they just, steady Eddy, keep their noses down and stick to it with the determination of a professional hit man, it gets you double agitated.

It was a Friday morning at the end of the bus ride when they made their move. Christy and Mary Ann were sitting hunched over with their feet in the aisle in the middle of the bus. The bookends, trapping Rose and me in the back of the bus a few rows in front of Luke.

I tried looking out the window, but they were like a magnet yanking my attention their way. At first all I could see was their massive bodies expanding and contracting like bulls waiting for the red flag. Then Christy turned slightly and mouthed words I couldn't make out. Mary Ann, puppy-dog style, copied Christy's movements exactly. But she added something of her own, which turned out to be the critical flaw in Christy's plan.

"Fuck you, white girl. Wait till you step off this fucking bus. We'll be there." Mary Ann bellowed so loud it reverberated throughout the bus.

Christy shot her an angry look and said, "Shut up, Mary Ann."

The small hairs on my arms bristled. Christy's plan had sprung a leak. Whether she liked it or not, Mary Ann had publicly announced the time and place, and Christy had to respond. If it had been up to Christy, the confrontation would have happened discreetly, spontaneously, and without a crowd, which would have been worse. I should have been relieved Mary Ann was such a bigmouth.

"Just step off this bus," Christy said in a slow, quiet, methodical voice, taking charge of the situation again after Mary Ann had screwed it up, "and you are going to be dead fucking meat."

Rose was ready. Her eyes popped open. She jumped to her feet and shouted back, "What did you say?" Her voice crackled through the now completely silent bus. "You saying something to us?"

"Outside, Rose," Christy snapped. The bus lurched to a stop and the kids began to file off as if the whole thing had been choreographed. "Just step outside. You won't be talking so tough in a few minutes." She shot her fist our way. "I've had it with you and your little white bitch."

The blood drained from Rose's face. My stomach flopped. This was it – open war. I walked down the aisle in front of Rose, barely able to take one step and then the next. My knees and ankles felt like water balloons; a loud buzz mounted up behind my ears. I was lunch meat. Lamb to the slaughter. My mind shot ahead. It was as if the dirty deed had already been done. I had been annihilated. I was floating in white space and echoes.

The kids had formed two lines at the bottom of the stairs of the bus. Everyone was ready and waiting to take their place in the drama. When we stepped to the ground, the crowd stopped talking and stared at us. Christy and Mary Ann stepped off the bus and stood directly in front of us, closing the lines at one end. The bus pulled away and kids shuffled behind us, forming a circle with Rose and me trapped in the middle. I looked frantically for Luke and Tim, but they were nowhere to be seen.

Before I could think, Christy pounced forward and snatched Rose by the jacket. Mary Ann grabbed my arm and dragged me toward the trunk of the oak tree. She pinned me against it, cop style – hands behind my back, feet barely touching the ground. I was limp and numb and my mind became a blotchy black screen of random noise. My knees and ankles collapsed and I sank into a pile on the ground, leaning partly against Mary Ann's legs. I heard Rose's voice but my head was making too much noise for me to decipher what she was saying.

"Keep your fucking mouth shut, you little bitch, and get your fucking white friend out of here." Christy's head shook, her cheeks wobbled, and her eyes, bugged and glassy, looked like they would bounce out of their sockets as she spoke. She shot Rose backward against the tree near my leg. Rose wasn't going to take it, there was no lie-down-and-die in that girl. She scrambled to her feet, ready for a faceoff. But before Christy had time to throw a punch, Luke and Tim stepped forward.

Luke reached down and, like a mother cat, grabbed the neck of my jacket, tearing me from Mary Ann's grip. Tim, Rufus, Denver, and Lionel stepped to the front of the crowd and formed a line facing Christy and Mary Ann.

The girls stumbled backwards and braced themselves against the tree. They looked like cheap, small-town thugs in a low-budget, no-account movie. Christy's cheek convulsed, causing a twitch in her left eye. Mary Ann's face looked like a dead cat's – glassy eyeballs in dry sockets, her lips stretched across her too-big-for-her-mouth teeth.

Maybe it was just my head playing games on me (God knows it hadn't been working too well that morning), but I was shocked at how small and young the girls looked.

Christy lowered her head. Luke didn't touch her, although he stood close enough for her to feel his breath.

"What are you doing?"

Christy's mouth was open, but no words came out.

"I said, what are you doing?" Luke wasn't really asking a question, but he waited for an answer.

Whatever fear I had left dissolved, giving way to embarrassment. Not for me – for them. I wanted to hide so I didn't have to watch their humiliation. The circle shifted until it became a crowd, everyone getting a spot to make sure they wouldn't miss anything. I was the only person who didn't want to see what would come next. I put my hands over my eyes.

Luke said it again, louder. "What are you doing?"

I moved a finger and opened my eyes a slit. I could see the whole thing: the accused, leaning against the tree, messed up and blank-faced afraid; the judges, hands on their hips, legs apart, facing the accused; the crowd, barely breathing, anxiously waiting their cue, ready to tar and feather or string the noose or gather the firewood. And the victims. Rose was ready; she'd shaken herself off and now her eyes were darting from Christy to Luke and back again. Me? I was a crumpled heap wishing I were invisible and that the trial were over.

Christy crossed her legs. Despite everything she'd done to me, I couldn't stand to see her pee herself. *Let them go. Forget the whole thing ever happened.*

Luke didn't flinch. Eyeball to eyeball, toe to toe he faced Christy. After a few seconds he stepped a body length away from Christy. In perfect sync, the crowd stepped back an equal distance.

"Christy. Mary Ann." He spoke each name slowly and punctuated them with his famous pause. "Rose is my friend. Josie is my family."

It was as if Luke had been waiting for this moment since he first heard about the girls threatening us, maybe even since Christy put the boots to Shelley. Now was his chance, and I doubt he could have imagined a more perfect scene in which to play his role of a lifetime.

"Look around, Christy. Look around, Mary Ann." Slowly he turned and pointed his finger from one kid to the next. Kids were standing there with their mouths open, mesmerized. "Do you see these people here?"

The girls froze.

"Do you see these people here?" Luke said again.

Mary Ann's head flopped up and down and Christy's swivelled loosely.

"Each person here is watching you." Luke didn't take his eyes off the girls. "If you touch one of these girls. . . "

He pointed to Rose and then to me. Neither Christy nor Mary Ann moved a hair.

"I said, if you touch one of these girls. . . "

Luke sounded like an orator, Martin Luther King or Gandhi. The crowd was paying attention to every word he was saying. It was so quiet you could have heard a hiccup.

"If you touch one of these girls, or if you touch any girl, or anybody, Christy, Mary Ann. . . " Again, he said their names with lingering precision. "If you so much as threaten to touch anyone, we will know. Someone will tell me or tell one of these guys and this crowd will come together again, and you won't get away as easily as today."

Luke turned from the crowd to face the girls again. "Understand?"

They flopped their heads.

"Understand?" Luke said. "I can't hear whether you understand or not."

"Yes." The word dribbled out of Mary Ann's mouth.

"Yeah," Christy blubbered.

"Good."

Luke swung around and walked toward the school. He pulled the crowd behind him like a magnet. I hung on to Rose's arm and stumbled ten steps behind. I glanced over my shoulder and saw Christy and Mary Ann still slumped against the tree; a small wet spot darkened the jeans between Christy's legs. They had got Luke's message, no doubt about it. I was glad it was over.

Chapter 10

After that Friday, the ocean between Rose and me disappeared for good. We were hip-to-hip friends for life. We didn't cut our fingers and become blood sisters or pledge on a Bible or do anything to prove it. That showdown had been enough to glue us together.

Rose doesn't remember it this way. I called her. I had to tell her about this crazy story I'm writing about a white girl on the reserve. She thinks I'm completely nuts. She's sure we were together right from the start, from the first bus ride. Other than Mom, of course; she remembers that part. She said I should stick to drawing perspective instead of writing about it. But before she hung up she made me promise to let her read the story when I'm finished.

Mary Ann seemed to instantly forget the whole bullying thing. By the next Monday she was like a long-lost friend. Whenever she passed Rose and me in the hall she called out, "Hey, cousin." She didn't hang out with Christy anymore. In fact, no one saw much of Christy at all. She only came to school a couple of times before Christmas, and after the holiday she never returned. They say she moved up north to live with her sister.

Which brings up Christmas. For the first time in years, I was looking forward to it. I didn't know what to expect, but it was going to be my first real family Christmas since Dad left.

When we lived in the city, Christmas for Mom and me meant one present for me (a sweatshirt or sweater usually) and one for her (a painted flower pot, although she didn't have flowers around the house, or a picture I had painted, or a picture frame that I'd made myself). Dad never showed up, and Mavis usually sent us some useless thing, "for the both of us," she'd say. For neither of us, more like it. One year we got a popcorn machine and another year she sent something that was supposed to make yogurt. We never even tried it out. Mom threw them in the closet until we moved, and then she chucked them out for good.

Mom usually cooked a Christmas look-alike dinner, basically just a frozen chicken already stuffed with breadcrumbs and onions. Her once-a-year cooking event. Her obvious effort but lack of delivery gave me an empty, pointless feeling about Christmas. What was the use of pretending for those of us who weren't going to get the mistletoe, silver bells, angels in the snow kind of holiday? Katy's place had Christmas, and so did Sarah's, but as for Mom and me, I would have been just as happy to skip it. So although I didn't know what Martin and Luke's Christmas would be like, I knew it couldn't be any worse than ours.

Two days before Christmas, Luke and I went shopping. Rose had been up north visiting her grandmother since school let out, and I was restless and bored. Martin gave us a list of things Grandma wanted bought for Christmas, and Mom gave me some money for a few presents, so we decided to go to the mall. Everyone must have been bored because at the last minute Mom and Martin decided to hitch a ride with us to the hospital to visit Grandma while we were shopping.

The thing about living forty minutes from town was that you never got to just say, Hey, I'm going to town. You had to plan it and organize. And if one person planned a trip, all of a sudden everyone wanted a ride whether they had it planned or not. Going to town became a great big event.

Luke drove, without his licence of course. Licences seemed to be optional on the reserve. They were something you got after you had been driving without one for a few years. Kind of like a diploma after you finished your practicum. Or for some of the more unlucky ones, a driver's licence was something you got after you got caught driving without it a few times and had too many fines to pay.

I had never been shopping with Luke. The whole idea of Luke and me in the mall seemed kind of strange. It was the same old place, although it felt like a foreign country. I was the same old person, but I felt like I was from outer space. And then to see Luke sauntering next to me – that was just too strange for words. And then, as if I wasn't feeling weird enough, what should happen? We walked through the front door of the mall, and just past the drugstore we almost bumped right into Sarah and Katy. They were sitting on a bench with bags piled around their feet. Their mouths fell open when they saw me, and I almost swallowed my tongue. I grabbed them both.

"Oh my God! It's so good to see you!" I gasped. I hugged and kissed them and couldn't let go.

When we finally settled down on the bench, Sarah stared at me while lifting her chin toward Luke as if to ask, Who's he?

"Oh, I'm sorry. I'm so rude," I said. "I didn't introduce you. This is Luke."

They stepped back and became instantly silent.

"Luke," I said, "this is Sarah and Katy, my very best friends from town."

He reached out and offered his hand. "Good to meet you, girls." He flashed them a wide smile.

Sarah might as well have seen a ghost. She never was one to hide her reaction when she saw a hot guy. And like her usual idiot self she threw a jerky hand out and grabbed Luke's. "Good to meet *you*." She turned to me and still with a gaping look on her face she flipped her chin toward Luke again as if to say, Are you really with this wicked hunk?

"Oh," I laughed. "No. I mean. . . He's not my. . . Oh my God, Sarah, he's my stepbrother."

That was all she needed to know. She jumped up and threw her arms around him. "Good to meet you, Josie's step-brother." She gave me a look. "Josie, you didn't tell me your stepbrother was," she paused, "like *that*."

Luke leaned back on another bench and sprawled his legs out. "Let me know when you're finished," he said and instantly fell asleep.

Katy and Sarah and I sat in a huddle, knees together, heads together (Sarah, of course, making sure she could keep her eye on Luke). For a few minutes it was like time travel: I was back in what used to be. Exactly like I imagined. Exactly what I had missed. Friends, the mall, shopping, it couldn't have been more perfect.

"Tell me everything," I said. "Everything."

Katy said she wasn't seeing her boyfriend anymore – I didn't know she had one. Sarah was trying to get Ryan – a guy I had never heard of. They partied Fridays and Saturdays usually at Rachel's place – I didn't know her either. Katy hated Mr. Arnold, her math teacher – no change there. And Sarah got an A in math – no change there. All I had to say was "Wow!" "Really?" "Great." Pretty soon the time travel started going the other way. It felt like it had been a hundred years since we had hung out. Who were these girls? Where did they come from? They lived in a different world, one I was no longer part of. Instead of listening to them talk, I found myself watching them as if I had just met them.

"What about you?" Katy asked. "What's been going on in your life?"

Now *there* was a question. Where would I start? Should I tell them about Christy and Mary Ann and how close I came to getting killed? Or that I liked a guy with braids who drove a seventies muscle car and looked like a gangster? I thought about my dreams of thin blue lights and the sounds of metallic cats crying in the night. How would that go over?

"Not much," I said. "Not much of anything exciting anyway. Just school and stuff."

"Do you *live* with that guy?" Sarah said.

"He's my stepbrother," I said. "I don't *live* with him."

"He's *so* hot," she said.

And then we ran out of things to say. It wasn't just them, it was me, too.

"We have to get together," Katy said. "I miss you, Josie."

"Yeah," I said. "I miss you too."

It was true. I missed them. At least I missed what I remembered about them. We hugged. I nudged Luke and woke him up. Sarah was all over him.

"God," she said. She wriggled against him. "It's been *soooo* good to meet you."

Sarah always made sure she got a piece of whatever guy was around. But it had never bugged me like it did that day. Maybe it was a brother-sister thing, but I couldn't wait to get out of there. When I left the mall I felt so out of it, which wasn't a stretch for me, but for once it wasn't about my colour or my race. It wasn't even Luke. I just didn't belong in their world anymore and there wasn't a chance in hell they'd fit into mine.

When we went up to Grandma's room to bring her stuff, the place felt more like a morgue than a hospital room. Mom was stiff as a board, lips almost blue from pinching them so tight. Martin held Grandma's hand and his forehead was covered in beads of sweat.

"It's okay, honey," Grandma said when they stood up to leave. "I'll be okay in the old folks' home. The doctor said it's a good place. It has good food and a nice little room with a view of the garden."

"Mom," Martin's voice cracked, "it'll only be for a few months. We'll get you set up at home. Really we will."

"Don't worry, son," Grandma said. She'd given up. There was no life in her voice and I wanted to cry.

Mom didn't flinch. She stood up, but it was like she wasn't really moving. This was real life, real people; Mom needed to make real decisions – a situation way beyond Mom's ability to cope. She had mentally checked out.

I wanted to scream at Martin, So much for Mom's stupid timetable. Looks like the hospital couldn't wait that long. There was no point screaming at Mom. She was almost comatose, and Grandma looked like she'd had enough disappointment for one day. So we dropped the bag on the bed, gave Grandma a kiss, and said, "See you on Boxing Day."

The next morning Martin and I were sitting at our usual places at the table, being unusually quiet. He interrupted the clink of our spoons when he said, "You want to help me bring some pots and pans up from the basement? And there's some old decorations we could pull upstairs if you want. We could make this place look like Christmas for the great Angus bash."

He laughed a little, as if there were a few stories he could tell about other Angus Christmas parties.

"Sure," I said enthusiastically. Finally I would get a chance to see what was down there, especially the space directly under my room, where the cats seemed to cry and where the blue light and the *No Trespassing* sign were making me crazy.

But Martin didn't get moving right away – maybe my enthusiasm had put him off. Instead he started listing off people who had been invited for Boxing Day dinner. Grandma was coming and a bunch of cousins and friends. Martin sounded pretty skeptical about whether his brother Arnie would show up, and he didn't seem to care one way or the other.

I asked, "You just got one brother?"

"Yeah," Martin said.

"Any sisters?" I said, thinking about the picture on the wall with two boys and a little girl.

"No" was all he said.

He got up, rinsed his bowl, left the room, and that was that. Nothing more about the pots and pans and decorations in the basement. And I wasn't about to push it. There were things about Martin that didn't add up – places in the house you didn't go – conversations that reached the end before they were finished. Living around here you just had to get used to leaving certain things alone. The basement was one and Grandma was another, and now it looked like I could add Martin's family to the list.

Chapter 11

It had been snowing on and off all week. The ground froze and snow piled up and by Christmas morning it was shin deep. We opened presents, played checkers and Scrabble and Monopoly, and ate scrambled eggs and salami. I'd never played board games and I wasn't much good at them. Luke won most of the time, but then he cheated every chance he got. If Mom got wind of him cheating, she'd stop the game and make a federal case of it, but other than that we had fun. Real family fun right out of a magazine, just like I imagined.

Boxing Day, the day of the Angus family Christmas dinner, was another story. People started arriving after noon. Cousins, uncles, friends – I'd met a few of them, others I'd never seen. Martin had prepared plates of cheese, Ritz crackers, pickles, smoked fish, oysters (which were totally gross and stank something awful), and salami. Women brought in trays of vegetables and fruit and crab cakes and stood in the kitchen with Martin.

To keep from getting bored I passed plates of food around to the guests in the living room. Do you want any more salami sausage? Crab cakes? Punch? There was no alcohol in the punch – Martin's orders – but it was pretty good anyway. Grandma shot commands my way if I overlooked anyone. More coffee for Max, she'd say and then point to the empty cup, or How about some more of those oysters for Lucy. I didn't mind; it made my job easier and that way I got to know everyone's name. Luke loaded logs in the fireplace and stuffed an old Bing Crosby Christmas tape in the player. "White Christmas" set the mood for what was shaping up to be a great party.

That all changed about five o'clock when the front door flew open.

"I'm here," a man hollered up the stairs. "The guest of honour has arrived." And then he laughed a totally fake *har-har-har* kind of laugh. I could tell before I saw him that whoever he was, he'd had way too much to drink. I stood against the wall and watched him stagger up the stairs.

"Blondie," he slobbered and made a beeline straight for me. "You must be the new adoptee around here."

He slapped me on my shoulder, too hard for joking. Then he stuck his cheek in my face like I was supposed to kiss him or something. God, I almost passed out from the smell of pot, beer, BO, and a whole bunch of stuff I couldn't even identify. I stepped out of his way and took a look at him. He wore a heavy wool knee-length coat, rumpled pants with holes at the knees, and shoes that turned up at the toes as if they were a size or two too big and maybe stuffed with newspaper. Everything about him was just a bit too big, too old, too worn, or too grubby. I'd seen guys that looked like him in the city, sitting on a street corner – sort of a Johnny Cash after he'd been dragged by a horse for a few miles look. He would have looked better, though, if he hadn't been so drunk.

"I'm Uncle Arnie, Martin's big brother, the family fuck-up. Har, har, har." When he opened his mouth to laugh I saw one front tooth and a gaping hole where the other one should have been. He eyed the room until he spotted Grandma and then hollered, "Ain't that right, Momma? I'm the family fuck-up. What do you say about that, nephew?"

I ducked around Luke and made a dash for the kitchen. Arnie followed and slammed two bottles of wine on the table.

"I guess you don't have a corkscrew, do you, sister?" he said, shooting a glaring look at Martin. His lips were wet and flabby. He stirred his words around in his mouth for a while before he spit them out. God, it was gross. You had to stand back if you didn't want a shower.

"No corkscrew around here." Martin faked a light, humorous voice, but I could see red blotches climbing up his neck.

"Don't you worry, girl," Arnie said. He was talking to Martin, and I could tell Martin didn't like being called "girl." "I can get into a bottle with my teeth if I have to."

He might have bitten the cork off the bottle. I didn't see. I ducked again and made for the other side of the living room, holding my breath over a full tray of oysters. I would have picked up something else if I hadn't been in such a hurry. The next time I saw Arnie he was sitting in Mom's spot on the sofa, glugging down red wine like it was Pepsi.

"Nice place you got here, sister," he shouted randomly around the room. "I guess your new family likes it here." He gulped the wine back until it was dribbling down his chin. "Yeah, I guess you got the house after all. I knew you would. Don't you worry, little Marty, Mom and I don't need a house. We're just fine."

People were doing their best to ignore him. An elephant was in the room and everyone was pretending it wasn't there. Even Grandma kept her back to him, cringing every time he spoke. After a while he got tired of hollering and slumped into the sofa with his chin on his chest. Just to be safe I kept my distance and refilled the cheese and crackers tray and punch glasses. Martin stayed in the kitchen preparing dinner, and, if you can believe it, Mom was helping. At least she made it look like she was helping. I think there were a couple of reasons other than helping that she stayed in the kitchen. First, Arnie wouldn't get out of her spot on the sofa. The other, more important, reason was that the women who brought the vegetables and crab cakes looked like they thought Martin was mighty interesting, and instinct told Mom to stick close to her man.

Martin called, "Dinner's ready," and we all filed up, one behind the other, at the table in the kitchen. The meal looked great. There was every Christmas food I could imagine: turkey, stuffing, bread, broccoli, Brussels sprouts, cranberry sauce, gravy – even a poinsettia in the centre on a white doily with candles on either side.

Martin stood at the end of the table. He must have forgotten about Arnie because he had a pleased look on his face, as if he had laid out a work of art. "Welcome, enjoy –" he began, and then Arnie really blew the lid off the party. He banged his bottle onto the table. Bowls and plates of food jumped. Arnie hammered his bottle onto the table again and shouted, "Nice spread, sister. Really nice spread you got here, all laid out just so like this."

He flung his arms across the table so dramatically that he knocked himself off balance. Before he hit the ground he grabbed the table with both hands and staggered back to a standing position.

"I want to propose a toast to the cook. The girl over here," he stammered.

Forget the smile on Martin's face. He looked like he had seen a ghost.

"To the woman of the house. Thanks." Arnie held his bottle toward Martin and then threw it back, splashing red wine over his chin and down his neck.

Grandma said, "Arnie, that's enough." Her face was as pale as Martin's.

"Oh, Momma." He turned and faced her. He was a total mess by then, red wine slopped down the front of his shirt and his pants barely hanging on to his hips. "I'm not quite finished. I want to thank your favourite son for inviting us to *his* house so we can meet his *new* family. I bet you're happy about that too, Momma."

No one dared take a breath. In an effort to get his act together, Arnie yanked up his pants, tucked in his shirt, brushed his hair back, and wiped his mouth (all this while holding or slugging back his bottle of wine). Then he wheeled around and stuck his face square in front of Martin's. Bloodshot and blurry-eyed Arnie slurred, "This place ain't yours, sister. It's mine and Momma's. You ain't got no right to be here. Not with that family of yours. Them white people don't have no right to be here."

A few women started shuffling around and edging their way to the door. You know the feeling – it was getting way too uncomfortable in the room and they had to get out of there. Not like Arnie gave a shit. He carried on without stopping. And part of me was glad, because he gave us more information about Martin's family in a few minutes' ranting at the dinner table than I had got in the past eight months.

Arnie said the house belonged to Grandma (like I had suspected) and that if she didn't live in it, the house was supposed to be his (news to me). "The old lady stays in the hospital, I got my street corner, and sister brings his new family home and cooks Christmas dinner," he hollered. "Hallelujah, sister. Thank you, Jesus, for Christmas, and God bless all of you." He waved his bottle like a madman, splashing wine everywhere. "What are you going to say for yourself, sister?"

Everyone looked Martin's way, hoping he would shut Arnie up, but he was speechless. So then Arnie started in on Martin himself, and that's where it got really interesting.

"You ain't so perfect, sister," Arnie shouted. "If Roy Jackson was around he'd still be after you for what you did to Tony. Putting him down like he was a dog. You think people just forget about stuff like that?"

I was all ears, expecting to hear some gruesome details explaining the scars on Martin's face and his jail time. But from the strained look on everyone's face, I think I was the only one.

Grandma rolled forward and took Arnie's arm. "That's enough, Arnie. You've had too much." More like we'd had too much.

Arnie ignored her and swung his bottle over her head, splashing wine on her dress and across a few of the people standing next to her. All of us stood frozen stiff around the table, which now looked more like the site of a food fight than a magazine cover. Mom's face was ghostly white. She leaned against the counter as if at any moment she was going to collapse on the floor. Martin looked like he was waiting to be hit by a car – frozen – a deer in the headlights. Grandma dropped her head and turned her back toward Arnie.

If Martin thought that by ignoring Arnie he would settle

down, he was wrong. Arnie wobbled and rebalanced. He sucked in a loud wet mouthful of slobber, ready to let loose again.

"And what about Ermaline?" he shouted.

Luke finally interrupted the moment and prevented what was lining itself up to be a complete disaster. He bolted forward and grabbed Arnie's arm. "Enough now, uncle," he said.

Arnie yanked his arm away and pointed from person to person.

"Are you guys going to let him do this to me?" he hollered. "This is my place, you all know it."

Luke grabbed his arm again and another man took his other arm. That was it. Arnie gave up and without any resistance he let them drag him down the hall to the bedroom.

As he left the room, he mumbled under his breath, "Sure. Leave Momma in the slammer for old people. You got a wife now, and a new kid."

Gradually people moved back up to the table, picked up spoons and forks and piled vegetables and turkey and cranberry sauce onto their plates. They said, "Pass the salt" and "Do you have any butter?" but not much else. Once their plates were full they sat on chairs in the living room. I pressed *repeat* on the Bing Crosby tape and turned up the volume to drown out the sound of chewing, swallowing, and the scratching of knives on china. A few minutes later Luke came out of the bedroom. All eyes were on him, everyone expecting him to give us a report or something. He kept his head down and walked through the living room without saying a word. The only thing I knew was that Arnie didn't appear for the rest of the night.

By eight o'clock all the guests had gone home except for

one couple who sat in the living room playing Monopoly with Mom and Martin. I was hot and bored and stuffed and needed fresh air.

"I'm going for a walk," I blurted out to Mom. "It's too hot and stuffy in here."

"Don't be too long," she said.

I couldn't believe my ears. She said "don't be too long" as if she'd been saying it for years. The truth was we had never had that simple a conversation once in our entire life. Anyway, she was preoccupied and I was out of there.

The sky was dark blue and covered with stars like a sheet full of Christmas lights. The air was clear and sharp in my throat but not freezing cold as I had expected. The moon cast a crystal light on the tips of the trees and glistened off the snow, lighting the road like a Christmas wonderland. I didn't know if it was the cold, the snow, the holiday, or what, but I didn't feel one bit afraid as I walked through the woods.

Halfway to the beach I heard wheels crunching through the frozen snow. Slowly a car rounded the corner and headlights cast a long shadow on the road in front of me. I kept walking without a flicker of fear, knowing what was coming. The car pulled up behind me.

"Hey," he said. "Want a ride?"

I glanced his way and then snapped my eyes away quickly. I only had time to catch a glimpse of his short-sleeved white T-shirt, identical to the one he wore the first time I had seen him.

"Aren't you freezing?" It blurted out of my mouth before I had time to think. So much for the smoothness I'd imagined.

He laughed. "I'm hot."

I had asked for it, but I wasn't up for joking. Embarrassed, I bent my head and hurried along.

"Slow down, Josie," he said. The way my name rolled off his tongue sent a vibration through my stomach and down my legs. "We can talk. It won't hurt."

I didn't slow down and he didn't say any more until we reached the beach. When I walked away from the road toward the logs, he turned his car off and jumped out to follow me. I brushed the snow off a log with my mitts and sat down. He used his bare hand and did the same. He sat beside me on the log, but far enough away so we didn't touch.

He rubbed his hands on his arms.

"You're freezing now," I said.

"Yeah, you happy?" he said. His teeth were chattering. "I'm freezing. How about we have this meeting in my car?"

I didn't answer, but I stood up and awkwardly walked to the car. I waited at the passenger door until he reached around my body and opened it. He didn't touch me, but an electrical current of his energy caught me in its arc and sizzled against my skin.

I fell into the seat – it smelled like old leather. Zeb jumped in behind the wheel, turned on the car, and fiddled with the heater. He rubbed his arms and hands until his teeth stopped chattering.

I was living out my daydreams, exactly. Well, not exactly. I was cool in my dreams. Now that it was for real, I was a complete klutz.

"Are you afraid of me?" he said.

A calm sort of turbulence was going on in my gut, just below my belly button. A slurry of warm and cold, like stirring soup, that made my hands shake. I pushed my palms up against my belly to settle down the outside and inside at the same time.

"No. I'm not afraid of you," I said.

I was surprised at how ordinary my voice sounded and that those words came out. I might have been telling the truth, but from what everyone had told me about Zeb, I was walking into a danger zone. My instincts weren't setting off alarm bells or caution lights. It wasn't fear I was feeling. It was a combination of a thousand things that I didn't have words for.

Zeb was all Indian. A little bit sleazy downtown Indian, a little bit Hollywood Indian, and a whole lot Johnny Depp kind of Indian. It was the Johnny Depp part that shook me up like a can of pop, fizz building up in my gut until I was ready to explode.

"What do you want to do?" he said. His body tilted slightly toward me to catch my answer.

What do I want to do? Do with what? Do with who?

"What do *you* want to do?" I said, thinking a question for a question was the easy way out.

He paused long enough for me to hear air flow out of his mouth and then back through his lips.

"I want to touch you."

Oh my God. My body convulsed into a mass of blubbering confusion. I wanted to laugh hysterically. Obviously he knew the sleazy part. I was creeped out. Who do you think you are? Elvis Presley? Buddy, get over yourself. I was turned on. Every crevice, every warm, out-of-the way place in my body vibrated and began oozing damp fluids. I was scared. What kind of touching did he mean? Just his hand on my arm would send me like a rocket through the roof. I was excited. He probably wanted to touch places no one had ever touched. The thought of being touched in those places was pure exhilaration. I was angry. How dare he manipulate me, get me in his car, and then attack me like this. I was dumbfounded. The feelings were bombarding me all at once. It was as if someone had thrown their dinner at me: turkey, stuffing, mashed potatoes, gravy, and everything. Should I lick my lips or wipe the mess off my face? Incoherent noises blathered in my head. Luckily they didn't come out my mouth.

Zeb moved his fingers and I stiffened. His hand reached forward and turned on the radio. The song was "White Christmas."

"Really," he said. "I want to touch you." He pulled his hand back and repositioned himself facing the steering wheel. "But I won't. Not unless you want me to."

I had no response for that. The guys I knew in town touched me whenever they wanted. I pushed them away if I didn't want to be touched. And if I'd had a few beers I might let them touch me a little, without thinking about it, and nothing big. And from my side – well, I had never been faced with this kind of tension. The kind of guy stuff I'd experienced was more like pawing a pet monkey than touching a live electrical wire.

"I want to be honest with you, Josie." He turned and faced me. He had slanting eyes, a wide mouth, high cheekbones, and large white shining teeth. Perfect features, other than a slight crook in his bottom lip as if it was swollen on one side. The kind of face I would have liked to paint.

"From the first time I saw you," he said, "I wanted to touch you. And talk to you. And get to know you."

"You mean that night at the youth centre?" I said.

"Yeah," he said. "Sorry for my stupid friends."

He shifted his body and rested his arm on the console that separated us. He had long thin fingers, groomed nails, and bony knuckles.

"Gordo is a full-out idiot. You should have seen him later. He got worse. I took off and left him."

"You don't need to be sorry," I said. "It wasn't you."

His fingers inched closer to my knee, which I had shoved up against the centre console to keep my leg from shaking. I could feel a cramp building in my calf, but I didn't move. It was as if every muscle in my leg was conscious of how close Zeb's fingers were.

The air was so thick in the car I could almost taste it. I gulped to give myself a second to think of something to say that would lighten up the conversation. "You from around here?"

"No," he said. "I'm from up north. My auntie lives here. Just across the highway."

"You go to school?"

"I quit. I'm finishing at Streetside, downtown, after Christmas."

"What grade are you in?"

"Twelve. Second time."

My mind was clear enough now to add it up. Grade twelve once – he would be about seventeen or eighteen. Grade twelve the second time – he had to be at least eighteen or nineteen years old. Mom would freak. Then I realized she was probably freaking anyway and that I'd better get home. Afraid to look like a little kid, I started figuring how I was going to tell him I had to go. Finally I got more afraid of what Mom would do than what Zeb would think and I just shot the words out. "I'd better go. They'll be wondering where I am."

Zeb lifted his hand, tapped my knee, and said, "I'll give you a ride home."

Instead of pulling his hand away, he left it on my leg,

burning a hole in my skin. He leaned forward, and without touching me he cupped his other hand around my chin.

"I like you a lot, Josie." He swept his fingers across my neck, connecting for just a millisecond. Then he leaned back in his seat. "I want to see you again."

What would Mom and Martin say? What would Rose say? Of course I couldn't see him again. It was impossible. "I. . ."

The word "can't" caught in my throat. I said, "Yeah, me too."

Yeah right, Josie Jessop. How the hell do you think you could get away with it? One thing I knew about the reserve was that everyone knew everything about everybody. Somebody had probably already seen us and was telling someone else; by breakfast Martin and Luke and Mom and probably everyone on the reserve would know I had been sitting with Zeb at the beach.

"How about tomorrow?" he said.

"Oh, I can't," I said.

"Why not?"

"Uh, I'm busy."

"Doing what?"

"I have things to do at home."

He met my eyes and squinted. The lie was so obvious it flapped around in the air between us. It's not going to work, Josie, no matter how hard you want to be cool, I thought.

I had to say it. "My mom would never let me see you," I said. "I'm only fifteen."

"I know," he said. "You're in grade ten and your mom hates Indians."

I felt the air seeping out of my lungs. I was a balloon with a slow leak, gradually shrivelling up into a wrinkly pile. Zeb was too big for me, too old, too cute, too experienced, too exciting, too dangerous. He was just plain too much and miles out of my reach. Why was I even sitting in his car talking to him? Whatever I had thought in a moment of infatuation was wrong, and I had to find a way to get out of there.

"I can't see you, Zeb," I said.

He said, "Don't say can't. I'll watch out for you. We'll talk later."

He pulled over to the side of the road at the turn near Martin's. I opened the car door and stepped into the crunchy snow.

"I'll see you again, later," he waved. "I'll watch out for you."

I shut the door gently. I waited until the rear lights of his car disappeared around the corner and then ran towards home, my feet barely touching the ground.

I'll watch out for you. I'll watch out for you.

When I entered the living room I braced myself. I was sure my face was flashing the news like a neon sign: Josie's been sitting in a car with a boy, no, a man. Mom was bent over the Monopoly board concentrating on her next move. I took a deep breath and prepared for her attack.

She glanced my way and said, "Did you have a nice walk, honey?" No one else paid any attention to me.

"Yeah," I said. "It's awesome outside. The snow. . . "

There was no need to continue. Mom wasn't listening.

Chapter 12

I remember thinking it was my blonde hair and the fact that I was white that made everyone on the reserve treat me weird. I thought they had a problem. A big problem. I knew Indians weren't the only ones who were prejudiced and racist. No one needs to be told that white people are racist against Indians, it's pretty obvious. I just never thought that I *was. When I moved onto the reserve, if anyone had said I was prejudiced, I would have denied having even a hint of racism in me. Mom did. I knew that. And Mavis did as well – hello, obviously, she didn't even try to hide it. But not me. I would have insisted that everyone was the same to me, no matter what colour.*

But now that I think about it, and especially now that I write about that first year on the reserve, I have to admit that I had my own issues about Indians. First of all I didn't, or maybe I couldn't, really trust Rose, not for a long time. I was afraid of her. I thought she would snap and turn against me. I excuse myself and say that I felt that way because I was self-conscious or something, but if I am really honest (and that's why I'm writing this), the reason I didn't trust Rose is because I didn't really trust Indians. Deep down I thought they were capable of anything – especially the bad stuff.

Then with Zeb it came up again. Only it wasn't just a little mistrust; it was full-out fear. When I lay in bed and thought about dating an Indian man, I was terrified on two counts.

The man part was pretty scary, no doubt about it, but the Indian part was totally terrifying. I wasn't afraid of anything I could put my finger on; it was everything in general. Maybe what Katy's mom said about Indians being dangerous stayed in my head. Maybe I believed her.

So now I'm pretty sure I had more to do with the way I was treated than I once thought. There's some truth to what they say – you get back what you give out. My blonde hair and white skin only made things worse.

Rain and wind whipped against the kitchen window. The weather had turned from freezing and snowy to windy and wet. Shrunken mounds of brown snow leached into the puddles at the edge of the road, giving the effect of water coming up as well as water pouring down.

I didn't care. My mind was set on seeing Rose. As I walked to the bus I had to sort out what to tell her and what not to tell her. Zeb was what I wanted to say, Zeb, Zeb, Zeb, but what would she think?

"Josie!" she hollered as she came up the stairs of the bus. "I got so much to tell you I don't know where to start." She flopped beside me and leaned her shoulder into mine. She swung around so we were face to face, almost nose to nose. "I missed you."

"I missed you too," I said.

Her face crinkled to one side as if she was making a decision.

"Okay, the very first thing in my head, Josie," she laughed, "the only thing in my head other than how much I missed you is. . . " she paused and giggled some more, "I met the cutest guy in the world."

She told me every detail of Jason. She said he was big, brown, and beautiful – the first three most important things about him. The next three most important things about him were he was a soccer star, smart, and sexy.

"No. Actually the very most important thing about him… " She stopped and then laughed. "It's his butt. You should see the way he walks. He is *soooooo* hot."

"Rose!"

"No, really, Josie." She lowered her voice. "You gotta see it."

"Oh, yuck," I said. "You sound like my mom."

"We didn't really get together," she continued, "not until the last day. He lives next door to my grandmother and we were all eyes for each other. Then the last day, just before I had to leave, he came over and asked me if I wanted to go for a walk on the beach. Just him and me together."

She looked out the window, glazed over, and let the fence posts and telephone poles whiz by without seeing them. "He kissed me."

She swung back around and almost crashed into my face.

"He kissed me, Josie. It was the most amazing kiss I have ever had in my whole life."

Rose described every steamy thing – his hands, lips, wet tongue, hard body, the smell of his breath, the hairs on his face.

"And for Christmas," she sighed and changed the subject, "Grandma gave me the down payment for a car. And Dad said he'd pay for the rest of it. Eight months and I'm sixteen. I'll have a car, Josie. We'll be able to do anything we want. Like going up north and seeing Jason."

Rose was spoiled beyond belief. Besides the new car she got new everything else, too: jeans, running shoes, jacket, purse, and tickets to the hockey game and a concert. "And… " Rose was ready to carry on. Then she paused, to the count of a quick two or three, sensing I had something to say. "What about you?"

I still wasn't sure what or even if I should tell her about Zeb, so I fidgeted with my zipper. I wanted to tell her about his long fingers (talk about sexy) and the smell in his car and the way he moved his lips and licked them with the tip of his tongue when he spoke. I wanted to ask her what to do about the mass confusion he stirred up in my belly. But although Rose and I had got close, I was still afraid of what she would think and that I'd kept a secret from her since I first met Zeb at the youth centre.

"Well, I didn't get a car for Christmas," I said. "Or as many clothes as you did." I got a sweatshirt from Mom, a DVD player from Martin (which was the coolest present I had ever got), and a card from Mavis. She said my present was a promise – she was coming to see us in the summer. I wasn't sure I believed her or even if I wanted her to come out.

"I got piles of stuff," she said. "Some of it doesn't fit me. You can come over and go through it. But what did you do? What happened?"

"Not much," I said. "No one kissed me."

She laughed and met my eyes. "No one?"

"It's true," I said. "No one kissed me except Grandma. But some stuff happened."

Rose waited.

I told her about Arnie and Boxing Day dinner and that Martin was going to clean up the basement so Luke could move downstairs. I told her about Katy and Sarah and how Sarah couldn't keep her eyes off Luke and mauled him all over when she said goodbye.

I felt a little guilty when I was finished. I had left out the most important part. I wasn't going to be able to keep Zeb a secret from her forever, not if I was going to see him again. But I couldn't tell without blurting the whole thing out, the youth centre incident and everything. Then she would know that I had been keeping a secret from her all the way along.

Rose, being the kind of girl who doesn't miss a thing and knows most things about most things, leaned against me. Her nose was only inches away. "Are you holding out on me, Josie Angus?"

"Josie Jessop, you mean," I said. "Holding out on you about what?"

She grabbed my hands. "I get the feeling that you're not telling me something. Tell me, tell me."

Tell her, tell her.

"I know something else happened to you over Christmas," she said. She didn't take her eyes off mine, "because I heard a little something."

Then I felt like a total schmuck. What did she know?

"I heard that you got a ride from Zeb Prince. He dropped you off around the corner from Martin's house," she said.

I squeezed her hands and looked into her face. She was about to burst with curiosity. Her eyes were wide open and looked like saucers of black ink. She was giddy, waiting for me to speak. Why was I afraid?

"Did he kiss you?" she prompted.

"You're crazy!" I exclaimed. "No, he didn't kiss me."

She didn't move. "Well?"

I swallowed and pushed giant lumps down my throat. If I had been honest in the first place this would have been a lot easier.

"He didn't kiss me," I started slowly. "But he touched me. His hand on my knee." I took her hand and placed her palm and fingers in the exact spot where Zeb's hand had been. I shivered as I told her how we met on the road on Boxing Day. I described the smell of the leather seats and how Zeb's voice sounded like the feel of a bubble bath.

"He's awesome," I said. "But he's nineteen, almost twenty, and everyone will flip."

I told her how tension between us hung in the air like a thick blanket holding him on one side of the car and me on the other. I described how tingly and wet I got all over when he put his hand through the invisible barrier and placed it on my knee.

"It was like I had sprung full of holes," I said.

After I finished telling her, she stayed perfectly still for a few moments and then threw her arms around me. "God, Josie," she said. "That was some story. You had me in suspense. There's a movie in that one."

She pulled back and cleared her throat. "If that's what you did over Christmas, then I got more I need to tell you. I got all kinds of stories about Zeb while I was up north. You better hear them."

It turned out Zeb used to live up the street from Rose's grandmother, with his older brother. Rose didn't know who his parents were, but they hadn't been in the picture since he was a little kid. Zeb's brother got busted for selling cocaine after a gang fight took place on the road outside his house. Rose's grandma called the cops, there was a full-out shoot-up, and ambulances carried people (including one cop) off to the hospital. Everyone who lived at the house and hadn't been shot got shipped off to jail in the paddy wagons, Zeb included. He was locked up for several weeks before the cops decided he wasn't part of the cocaine deal.

Apparently he had been just about to graduate. When all hell broke loose at his brother's place, his auntie invited him to move down to the reserve and live with her so he could finish school.

Rose paused long enough for me to try and digest what she had just said.

Then she said, "He was raised like a gangster, he looks like a gangster, but maybe he's not a gangster. Now all we have to do is convince Martin and Luke that he's not a gangster."

"And," I said, "we just have to convince Mom that he's sixteen."

There was more. Zeb and Jason were good friends. Jason had been the one who told the police Zeb wasn't into cocaine. He got Zeb off the hook.

"They're friends, we're friends. . . " Rose was giddy with excitement. "It's going to be so great. We can all go out."

"Wow, hold on," I said. "We're not even together yet, and Jason's in another city."

Rose was not about to be held back by small details.

"We're going to have so much fun," she said as if she didn't hear what I'd said.

When I got home from school, Martin was hauling boxes into the backyard.

"You want to help?" he hollered.

"Sure."

Around the back he said, "You want to feed this stuff to the fire? There's lots of dry paper and cardboard."

Martin had thrown boxes and loose bags of paper garbage on top of the muddy and sopping wet mound of garden debris. I scrunched up a few sheets of an old newspaper and lit it on fire. Soon flames shot up into the air and red-hot embers sizzled their way through the surface of the burn pile.

Martin dragged the junk to the pile and I fed it to the fire. Magazines, newspapers, cardboard boxes that had held running shoes or chocolates. They had saved everything. Now I fed it to the fire and the flames gobbled up the garbage.

"Don't let it get away on you," Martin said.

"This all from the basement?" I asked, keeping my eyes on the fire.

"Yeah," he said. "It's a new year. Time to move on. Mom's gotta get out of the nursing home."

"Isn't she getting tired of waiting?" I said, my anger at Mom and Martin building for letting Mom get in the way for so long.

"It'll be soon," he said. I could tell he wasn't convinced when he added slowly, "And that will be the right time."

I'd never argued with Martin, but I'd never wanted to so badly either. What was such a big deal? Why didn't he just tell Mom that Grandma was coming home and it wasn't up to her? Then a thought flashed through my head. Maybe it wasn't all about Mom. Maybe Martin had issues of his own.

Chapter 13

You don't know what you don't know. It's as plain as that. You might have an idea that there is something fishy happening, a feeling that you can't quite put your finger on. But if you don't have the information, you just can't know what's up. And another thing – you never know where the information is going to come from. That was the thing about the room downstairs. One of my first clues that things were really weird with that room was that Martin and Luke didn't like to talk about it. I felt their mood change when the room was mentioned. The other thing was that no one went into the basement. The whole family stayed upstairs all the time. When Martin asked me to go down and get the pots and pans at Christmas he took those words back as fast as he said them.

Then, of course, there was the blue light around the window and the images of No Trespassing *when I was asleep and maybe when I was awake (I was never sure). Not being a fan of stuff you can't explain, like dreams and visions, and not getting any answers from Luke, I put it into the back of my mind. Like the sounds – the crying that sounded like a cat in a tin can? Well, I just put it down to a cat. And the hot ankles? Some weird duct thing. As for my own feelings, when I stood at the basement door and couldn't convince my hand to grab the doorknob – well, that was just another case of the gutless wonder at work. So it all kind of filtered around the edges of my mind, waiting for something to make sense of it.*

It's not until you put it together and look at something all at once that you say to yourself, Why didn't I know that before? That's when you decide to trust your senses and begin to listen to the things you feel, even if they seem to be coming from outer space. That's where perspective comes in. It's when you see a thing from all angles that you can really get a handle on what the thing is. But then, knowing builds on itself. You get to know one piece at a time until finally you say, Aha! I get it now!

And just a note here in case you were wondering what was happening to Grandma. We visited her, almost every week. The nursing home wasn't any better than the hospital. It smelled the same and the room was just as dingy and little. The only improvement was that instead of looking out onto a parking lot she now had a garden view, which I think got a little boring for her. When we visited, everyone in the room had a silent agreement. No one said one word about when she was moving home. After what Arnie said at Christmas, the subject was dropped like a hot potato. Even Grandma seemed to be part of the agreement.

I, of course, wanted to fight about it, but what could I say?

When Martin did spring cleaning, it seemed he started with a New Year's resolution and then didn't really start working until the spring. Although I often heard the sound of shuffling and scratching coming up through the heat vents, it didn't appear to be Martin cleaning up down there. I didn't hear a word about the basement until Luke's birthday.

On February 4, Martin said to Luke at the breakfast table,

"Happy birthday, son. By spring break we'll have the old room downstairs cleaned out and you can move your stuff in."

"You got it, Dad," Luke said. "But I think Grandma's the one who must be getting impatient. That old folks' home sucks."

Martin said, "We'll get her home soon."

Yet it wasn't until a month after Luke's birthday, a week before spring break, that Martin actually got back to work on the basement. After school I rounded the corner and saw Martin sitting on the front porch. His back was to me, his butt was hitched up on an old tire on the concrete, his elbows rested on his knees, and his chin was hanging in his hands. There was a hammer and crowbar leaning against the porch next to his feet.

"Hey, Martin," I called. Surprised. I didn't expect to see him sitting on the porch looking, even from behind, like he was bummed out. "What's up?"

"Blondie," he said. I had gotten used to the way Martin said Blondie. In fact I was beginning to like it. He laughed. "Not much."

I dumped my sack on the ground and plunked my butt next to his.

"What are you doing?" I said.

"I have one week to get that basement cleaned and ready to go for Luke. I set myself a deadline," he said. "And I haven't started on that old room." He tossed his nose over his shoulder in the direction of the boarded window.

"I thought I heard you down there the other night," I said.

Startled, he pulled his chin back and gave me a quick look from under his bent eyebrows.

"What did you hear?"

I thought about what Luke had said about woo-woo stuff and decided to keep it light.

"Oh, nothing, just noises," I said. "Probably the furnace."

"Are you sure?" he said. "The furnace isn't at that end of the house."

"It was probably nothing at all," I said. "I'm always hearing and seeing things."

Silence. Martin dropped his chin into his hands again and jiggled his foot. The room stood between us like an elephant in our conversation. I wasn't telling him what I was thinking and I was sure he was holding back on me, too.

Eventually I blurted out, "I think that room's kind of weird."

Martin's back stiffened. He lifted his head and said, "How do you mean, weird?"

"Well, like, you don't want to work in it, do you?"

Without answering he nodded his head for me to continue.

"And, well, I really did hear noises a few nights ago. And other times too. It's not the furnace. And. . . " I said and paused. That's all you need to say, Josie, I told myself. Leave it alone.

But Martin said, "And? And what?"

"And. . . well, sometimes I see a thin blue light around the windows. In my dreams. At least I think it's in my dreams."

"And?"

"I've seen a weird sign."

"A sign?"

By then Martin's face had perked up and he was watching every word as it came out of my mouth.

I said, "It's a *No Trespassing* sign. At least that's what it looks like. Nailed to the window. It fades in and out in the dark but isn't there at all when it's light out."

I stopped talking. Martin's eyes stayed fixed to my mouth.

Then I said, "I don't know why I'm telling you this stuff, because it sounds pretty stupid."

"It's not stupid, Josie," he said. His eyes were almost drilling holes in my face – I couldn't look at him.

He did something then that he hadn't done before. He shuffled his body closer to mine and put his arm around me. He leaned against me until his mouth was next to my ear. In a half whisper he said, "Josie, I need to tell you something." Then he stopped talking for a minute, maybe two. It felt like an hour. Barely breathing, I stayed perfectly still.

"I need your help," he said. He stood up. "Come with me."

Picking up the hammer and crowbar, he motioned to me with his chin to follow him around the side of the house and into the basement. Lit only by the open door, the room was dark and it smelled like a bathroom laundry hamper. Blankets covered two small windows on either side of the large room. It had a rough concrete floor and a couple of posts holding up the ceiling. The beams and walls were exposed and unfinished. Martin flicked on the light and I could see the room was almost completely bare except for a few boxes stacked against the far wall.

"Over here." He pointed to a faded red door in the wall to our right.

We walked a few steps and stopped a body length away from the door.

"That's the old room, there," Martin said.

I moved closer and reached to open the door. Martin threw out his arm and held me back like a mother holding her kid out of the traffic.

"Not yet," he said. "I need to tell you first. It's time."

I began to shiver from the damp feeling in the room. I moved closer to Martin and rubbed the goosebumps off my arms. After a few moments he leaned his hammer and crowbar against a post. He stepped up to the wall next to the door, pressed his back against it, and slid down until his knees hit his chest and his butt sat on the floor. Like a little kid.

"Come here." He tapped the floor beside him.

I slid down the wall next to him until we were sitting shoulder to shoulder.

"I have to tell you, Josie, it's no good to have secrets. Stuff happens, it hurts, it sucks, and you bury it. That's what I do anyway. I bury stuff and pretend it didn't happen. I get on with life. Put a smile on my face. All that good stuff that made a man out of me."

God, Martin, this is heavy, I thought. New territory for me. I didn't know whether he was talking man to man, father to daughter, or friend to friend, but I knew no adult had ever talked to me like that before. What he was saying was coming from so deep inside I felt like I was trespassing on private property. Even though Martin was inviting me in.

"I shut the door on the stuff I didn't like. And you see that door right there?" He motioned toward the door. "I shut that door twenty-five years ago and I haven't opened it since."

What was I supposed to say? My legs began to cramp something horrible, and pain shot up my back. Any small movement made it worse, but I stayed perfectly still.

"Now I have to open the door. Mom's coming home. Luke needs a room. But the real reason I have to open that door..." He shot a look at the door as if he was mustering courage for a full-frontal attack. "It's just fucking time I got over the stuff that happened in that room." His voice grew deeper. "It's fucking time, Josie."

I was shocked to hear Martin swear. He had never used that word before, or any other swear word as far as I could remember.

I said the obvious thing. "What happened in that room?"

He began to crawl like a spider up the wall until he was standing. He reached out his hand and pulled me up beside him.

"I'll show you."

When he slowly stretched his hand toward the handle, it looked like a magnetic force was holding him back. He bit his lip and frowned when he grabbed the knob, turned it, and pushed the door open just a slit.

"This won't be pretty, Josie."

He grabbed my arm and leaned against me. I shuffled beside him as he opened the door further and entered the room. A waft of damp mouldy air hit my nose. The room was dark except for a few thin streaks of light that streamed in around the edges of the boarded windows. Martin reached behind me and flicked on the light.

"Oh my God," I said. Martin's knees buckled and both of us fell against the wall.

A piece of white rope, shaggy at the end, hung in the centre of the room. A wooden chair lay on its back a body length away and the walls were spattered with graffiti. Martin pulled a knife from his pocket, stood the chair up under the rope, stepped on the chair, and sliced the knot away from the beam. He bunched the rope in his hands and handed it to me. Then he picked up the chair, walked out of the room, and grabbed some newspaper from a box in the basement. I followed him into the backyard where he scrunched the paper and tossed it on the burn pile. He tossed the chair on top, motioned for me to do the same with the rope, and then lit the paper on fire.

As we stood side by side watching the flames burn up the suicide tools, Martin said, "My baby sister. She was seventeen years old. I was twenty-eight. I came home one day and found her. She was such a pretty girl. She always smiled, not like me and Arnie. She was a flower, we were weeds."

Martin spoke short sentences between long pauses, letting out bit by bit what he had kept hidden for so long.

"Mom was gone. Years in the hospital. TB. Arnie was drunk. Or stoned. It was just me and her." There was an unusually long pause. "Ermaline. I promised Mom that I would take care of her. I didn't. I didn't pay attention. I didn't know she was so sad. I lifted her down and carried her out of the room. I shut the door. I never came back to the room. Or the basement if I could help it. I drank myself stupid, did time, drank myself stupid, did time, messed someone up for good, did more time. When I finally sobered up I kept the door shut on this part of my life."

Martin talked about the afterlife. He said Ermaline was happy now. He could never be sure before. He said her round eyes turned down at the corners making him think she was sad even when she was laughing. He said she was tiny like me and she loved to sing.

"She had a voice like a bird in the spring," he said. "She made up her own songs, words, tune, and all."

We turned back to the house.

"Will you come back in the room with me?" he said. "I didn't read the words on the wall."

"Are you sure?" I said. "It'll be kind of hard."

"Hard is okay, Josie," he said. "Avoiding it hasn't been easy. Now it's time to face it."

He rested his arm on my shoulder and walked through the basement. We stopped at the door. "You don't have to come in," he said. "I wasn't thinking about you, I'm sorry."

"No," I said. "I'm here for you. I just can't imagine. She wasn't much older than me."

In the far corner of the room was a single bed with brown metal head- and footboards and a shiny pink flowered bedspread. Two pairs of black shoes and a pair of fuzzy pink slippers were placed in a perfect line on a small terry-towel mat at the foot of the bed. A large dresser with fancy drawer pulls and curlicues around the mirror stood near the window. Placed neatly on top were hairspray, perfume, a brush, a wooden jewellery box, a blue china bowl, and a windup clock with the hands stopped at quarter to twelve.

On the wall opposite the bed hung a pink housecoat and bulky blue jacket next to a poster. The picture was a seventies rocker guy with long curly blonde hair, a wild-looking guitar, and a bare chest. Under the picture it said *Peter Frampton.*

"I gave her that poster," Martin said. "She loved Frampton."

The room was in perfect order, other than the walls. They were covered in felt-penned words, some scrawled messily and others printed as precisely as if they had been done by a grade-school teacher, ruler underneath and all.

You see me smile
You think I'm happy
You see me get good grades
You think I'm smart
You see me do as I'm told
You think I'm well behaved
You don't see me cry
So you don't think I'm sad
You don't hear me shout
So you don't know I'm angry
You don't see my brain
So you don't know I'm crazy
I'm an alien, from outer space
I have green hair, four nostrils, one eye, six legs, three breasts with giant nipples
So you all can suck like babies
Don't touch me or I'll kill you

Scrawled in large letters, as if it was added as an afterthought, was

Don't touch me or I'll kill me.

Underneath was written

The world spins too fast

More words were scribbled underneath but I couldn't read them. She must have done it in the dark because each line had been written on top of the others until it was a pile of dark ink.

We inched our way around the room. Words were flung across it as if she had spit them out of her mouth. I AM NOT WHAT YOU THINK I AM, I AM NOT, I AM NOT, I

AM NOT, I HATE YOU, I HATE ME, YOU HATE ME, YOU HATE YOU, I HATE THE WORLD, THE WORLD HATES ME.

We stepped sideways slowly as if we were in a museum, pausing at each inscription as if we were examining an ancient exhibit. After each message Martin leaned more heavily on my shoulder. Under the window near the foot of her bed was a poem written with a blue pen. In places where the pen had dried up, the words faded and almost disappeared. Then, as if she had shaken the ink back to the tip, the words were once again bold and readable. It was done in beautiful handwriting. It looked like after she assaulted the walls with the thick red felt marker, she quietly picked up her pen and wrote her final message.

I'm sorry Mom
I'm sorry Martin
I tried to be okay
But I'm not
My brain screams ugly things
I can't stop it
It won't stop
I have to stop it
Please forgive me
Please forget me
Your little girl, Ermaline

There was a line of X's and O's under her name and a big heart filled in until the red ink had run out.

Martin's eyes glazed over as he stared at the figures as if they were hieroglyphics. Drained of air and blood and the will to see any more, he sank in a heap on the floor. He pulled his knees to his chest and I watched his body heave.

It was quiet except for the sucking sounds of long streams of air being drawn in through his nose. Then low primal moans, half animal, half machine-like, came from his belly. I kneeled next to him, not knowing what to do with him or the scary pain that was turning over in my gut. For twenty minutes or maybe an hour or two – I couldn't tell – I stayed next to him, frozen. Gradually Martin became silent until finally he lay perfectly still on the floor. His skin was grey and stretched like plastic wrap over his face, or like the skin of a dead man. His lips were tight thin strips of purple. Eventually even the flicker in his eyes became still and I put my hands on his chest to check to see if he was still breathing. Barely. There wasn't much I could do. I thought about getting out of there but I knew that was stupid. I couldn't leave him there alone.

Finally his eyelids slowly separated, exposing yellowish hollow cavities where his eyeballs appeared to float in space. When we scrambled to a standing position, Martin turned out the light and shut the door behind us. He picked up the hammer and crowbar, and I followed him out the basement door.

"Here," he said.

He passed me the hammer. He took the crowbar, yanked the plywood off the back window, and tossed it on the burn pile. We walked to the window at the front of the house and did the same thing. It was getting dark by the time the wood had burned up.

When I got home from school the following day, two women sat with Martin at the kitchen table. One looked like a gypsy fortune teller or someone who reads palms or tarot cards. She had a loose white ponytail tied with a woven scarf and wore an orange sweatshirt with a green and blue and purple parrot appliquéd on the front, and long metal earrings that sounded like wind chimes when she moved her head. The other woman was old, maybe as old as Grandma. She sat with her hands folded across her massive chest. She lifted her eyes and nodded her head when I entered the room. Martin introduced them as elders from the community.

"They've come to clean out Ermaline's room," he said. "I should have had them come twenty-five years ago. It's something our people do when people die. Cecelia and Anne will take all Ermaline's stuff and burn it. They will pray and use cedar boughs and water to cleanse the room. When they're finished they'll use smoke and herbs and cedar to cleanse us too."

I locked my bedroom door. After a few minutes I heard the women begin a slow eerie cry; then I heard bells ringing, and pretty soon the cries turned into high-pitched wails. I watched them light a fire in the yard and stand facing the flames, lifting their hands to the sky. They prayed in a language that sounded more like chants than words. Martin pulled the dresser and shoes and housecoat and ski jacket to the side of the fire. The old woman kept her hands raised to the fire and prayed while the younger woman and Martin tossed the things into the flames. They stayed until the last ember went out.

Martin called me to the living room and we lined up – Luke next to Mom, and me on his other side. The old woman crumbled dried herbs into a large abalone shell. She flicked a lighter and held the flame to the herbs until a thin trail of smoke curled up to the ceiling and a thick pot smell stung my nose.

She held the shell up to Mom's chest while the other woman waved her hands and cedar boughs until clouds of smoke billowed around Mom's body from her head to her toes. Mom was standing stiff as a board with her hands frozen at her sides and her chin poking out toward the women. Her face was expressionless and her eyes were fixed on the far wall as if the women were invisible. And she was holding her breath, her cheeks puffed out like little balloons ready to burst. It looked like an endurance test – if she didn't breathe, maybe she would survive. If the whole thing wasn't so darn serious I'm sure everyone would have laughed. Mom relaxed a little and caught her breath when the women moved on to brush Luke.

When the smoke surrounded me, my body relaxed. I took a deep breath, expecting some kind of mystical experience, maybe a vision or voices. I would have liked an explanation – why the blue light? What about the *No Trespassing* sign?

But I felt nothing, not even a buzz. No woo-woo stuff at all. They brushed off Martin and then each other. When they were finished, the old woman licked the end of her fingers and pinched the burning sage.

Once the smoke cleared the old woman moved back in front of Mom. "This is for you," she said and pulled the perfume decanter from her apron pocket. She handed it to Mom.

She gave Martin the jewellery box, Luke the bowl, and she hung a long gold chain around my neck. On it was a small gold heart with tiny hinges. The woman's old fingers fumbled with the pendant until it sprang open. On one side was a picture of Martin when he was about fifteen years old, and on the other was a picture identical to the one on the living room wall – of the chubby little girl with the smile on her face.

Chapter 14

In a million years I could never have imagined what happened to Ermaline or all the pain that Martin and Grandma and Arnie must have suffered because of her. But once I entered the room and read her poems, I felt like I knew her. I felt like I knew the others better as well. I don't think it had the same effect on Mom. She didn't go downstairs until Martin painted the walls, and when I told her what Ermaline had written, she shut me up. "That's too morbid, Josie," she said. Which surprised me. Mom was one who liked to watch gruesome stuff on TV and talk about it. But Ermaline was real, and I guessed real was something Mom liked to avoid if at all possible.

They are right what they say about things coming to people who wait long enough (or something like that). Martin was right – it wasn't time for Grandma to come home until it was time. Time had a different meaning on the reserve. Martin always made jokes about Indian time, which meant that people arrived whenever they got there – ten minutes late, an hour late, a day late. But that's not how it was around Martin's place. We weren't late for things like the school bus, and Luke was never late for soccer practice. Martin was precise about what time we had breakfast and supper – the same time every day. So it wasn't so much the clock time that was different; it was how the people moved through their day, through their own lives. I got the feeling that I was moving with a current, on a river, or with the momentum of a train that didn't depend on me to get there. At Martin's you were part of a flow – the action wasn't all up to you.

It's hard to explain, but it's one of the most important things I figured out on the reserve and it's so important to my paper on perspective. It's about where you get placed, and then it's about where you place yourself once you are there. And it's about how much control you think you have on what's going on around you.

Zeb could help me out with this one. He's working with the kids on the reserve. He'll be out to visit me in two weeks and I can't wait. He'd say that the most important thing to learn in life is to find your rhythm and then figure out how it fits into the music that's playing around you. "Just let it flow, Josie," he says. "If you get too stuck on your own stuff you'll lose your beat. If you get too stuck on everyone else's stuff, they'll drown you out." And I have to say that after being around him for the past three years, I agree. I don't always live life like that, but in terms of perspective, I think he's got it right.

After Christmas, my meetings with Zeb became regular events. Every evening I told Mom I was going for a walk, and for some amazing and yet-to-be-explained reason she started saying yes. Every time. As long as I wasn't gone for more than an hour, she didn't say a word. I had no idea what Martin or even Luke thought about my "walks." They never asked, and I never brought it up when they were around.

Here's where timing was really important. I left the house about 7:15 and walked up the road through the woods.

Within minutes of me turning the corner, Zeb showed up. We drove to a beach off the reserve, parked in an old campsite, and talked. That was it. Once in a while we picked up Rose and we all drove to the gas station up the highway. We bought Slurpees or milkshakes and got home in time to keep Mom happy.

After a few meetings I figured out how to talk to Zeb without babbling. Just to keep safe, I didn't say too much. I kept my sentences short, nodded and smiled a lot, and usually got out a yes or no in the right places. I had to. He created turbulence and I had to maintain control or he would have thought I was a complete bimbo.

At times neither one of us would say a word. We'd listen to the radio under a cloud of tension that hung over us as if it was gravity, pushing him to one side of the car and me to the other. Zeb's hand was the only thing that crossed the centre line. He rested his arm on the console and rested his hand on my knee or my shoulder. Trust me – that was exciting enough. I don't know what I would have done if he had tried anything else.

Zeb talked about movies (usually ones I hadn't seen), sports teams (which I didn't know anything about), and TV shows (ones I might watch if Martin would hook up the cable in my room). We did the same thing every time. He'd pick me up safely out of sight of Martin's house, we parked safely out of sight of the reserve, we talked about something safe and stayed safely on our separate sides of the car.

It all worked out until the night after the women cleansed the house. I had missed meeting Zeb the night we opened Ermaline's room, so we hadn't seen each other for two nights. We met at our usual place and usual time, but that was all that was usual about that evening. It was as if a dam broke and washed away the gravity that kept us safely separated.

"Hey," he said when I jumped in the car. "What have you been smoking?"

What kind of question was that? I didn't smoke.

Zeb leaned forward and peered in my face.

"Are you all right?" he said. "You look like you've seen a ghost."

Nice talk. I didn't feel like being funny, but that was all it took to open the floodgates.

"You won't believe what I have to say, but I have to talk to someone," I said.

Instead of driving off the reserve, Zeb pulled up to the beach in full view of the road, turned off the car and the radio, and leaned toward me with his ear next to my lips.

I told him about my dreams, the lights, the cries, the floor, the *No Trespassing* sign. I told him about the room downstairs and Martin and Ermaline and the writing on the walls. I told him how Martin lay on the floor and I wondered if he was dead. Words bubbled up my throat and spewed out my mouth. There wasn't time for them to get mixed up and there wasn't any way for me to hold them back.

"And then last night I wasn't here because two women came and cleansed the house and us with sage and cedar boughs," I said. My mind cleared and all of a sudden I became embarrassed. What had I said? What would all that babble sound like to him? He would think I was completely nuts.

Self-consciously I said, "Wow, I thought I was fine after the cleansing. I'm sorry. I don't know why I said all that stuff to you. I'm sure you don't want to hear all my junk."

He waited, with his eyes gently resting on my lips.

I wasn't finished. I told him how I felt when the smoke covered my body. How I had hoped for voices or visions or at least some explanation, but all I felt was a peaceful glow around me. I showed him the locket and the pictures inside. I told him that the old woman said I was meant to come and live on the reserve – that all things happen for a reason – and that I shouldn't feel out of place.

The words formed their own waterfall. There was no stopping them, and when I finished talking I started to cry. Snivelling and sobbing, with streams of snot running down my nose that I had to keep wiping on my sleeve, I told him how it felt at first to be called Blondie. I told him about Christy and Mary Ann and how scared I was of everyone on the reserve – how sure I was that they hated me. I told him about Rose and how hard it had been to become friends. He passed me a napkin and I blew my nose. I said I hated the way Mom was and how she thought Martin was the only good Indian. I told him she was prejudiced and I hated it. Then I told him how much I liked the reserve now, even though it was the craziest place I had ever been in my whole life.

When I finished talking I was leaning across the gearshift. My head was pinned between Zeb's shoulder and chin, both his arms were around me, and the gearshift was poking me in the side. The waterfall had dried up, no more words and no more snot. My brain was quiet and the only sound I heard was Zeb's breath, in and out against my cheek.

"I'm sorry," I said. "I can't believe I didn't shut up."

"Wow, Josie," he said. "Don't say you're sorry. You don't have anything to be sorry about."

He was right, and the truth was, I didn't feel sorry either.

Other than the sharp pain where the gearshift stabbed me, I felt wonderful. I was exhausted and empty, but it felt good. It felt like I had taken off one blanket after another until I was free and light and loose and breathing fresh, uncluttered, unstuffy air.

Zeb squeezed me and pulled me closer. I manoeuvred my side just enough to ease the pain. "God, I wish it wasn't like that," he said.

"What?" I said.

"I wish we didn't do things like that around here," he said.

What was he talking about? The cedar boughs, the old women, the burning? Or was he talking about the white/Indian thing?

"Indians kill themselves more often than anyone else in the country," he said. "Did you know that?"

"No," I said.

"Yeah, well, it's not such a great thing to know." Zeb tightened his grip on my shoulders. "It's one of our favourite coping strategies. We hurt, we drink, we shoot cocaine, we hurt some more, we drink some more, shoot some more cocaine, and by that time we hurt so much, we hurt someone else. Turns out in the end we are all looking for a way out. And we hurt ourselves. Hurt people hurt people. Someone hurt Ermaline, she hurt everyone by killing herself..."

Zeb didn't finish his sentence. He buried his face in my hair. I heard him sob, or maybe I felt it. It was quiet for a long time and then he told me about his mother and father. He was seven years old. He was playing with his brother in the living room when they heard a shot in the basement.

"I knew right then," he said. "Even though I was just a little kid. I knew that shot meant something wicked had happened. Me and my big brother just kept playing. I looked at him thinking he would take me downstairs to check it out. He didn't. He kept playing. It was dark by the time he grabbed my arm and dragged me down the stairs. He switched on the light and there was my mother in a heap on the floor and my father hanging just above her."

Everything that had happened to me seemed so stupid and trivial when I imagined Zeb at seven. God, what did he do?

"Now my brother's on the same treadmill." Zeb's voice got slow and deep. "He got hurt. Now he's at the shooting cocaine, hurting people stage. Pretty soon he'll be looking for a way out. The permanent stage."

I felt like I was being swallowed by a black hole. I was free-falling, never hitting the bottom, but already eaten up by something very very dark. My dreams, the lights, the crying, the old house, Ermaline, Zeb, his mother and father, Zeb's brother – all swirled around me like junk in a whirlwind.

"It's a rotten, gross, unfair, useless cycle we are on." Zeb pushed himself up and then hung his arm on my shoulder. "It started more than a hundred years ago and it's still going on."

He grabbed the sleeves of my jacket and positioned me in front of him. It was as if it was the first time in the conversation he was talking directly to me.

"I'm going to break the cycle," he said. "That's what I'm about. I'm not going to hurt people, shoot up, drink, hurt people, shoot up, and end up hurting myself."

He looked at my eyes.

"Martin doesn't have Ermaline anymore," he said. "But he's got you."

His eyes softened, his tongue curled over his bottom lip, then he sucked his lip under his teeth. He stared at my face. I watched the subtle movement of his eyes looking at my eyes, nose, ears, cheeks, and then he fixed his gaze on my lips to the count of four or five and even longer, until my bones and blood were vibrating so out of control I could hardly sit still. Slowly he closed his eyelids and moved his face closer to mine until he placed his damp, slightly open lips on mine.

God, the kiss lasted, I don't know, maybe five minutes. It was the kiss of a lifetime – everything I had dreamed it would be. In fact, it still feels like a dream. When I think back I can't be sure if the kiss was really that awesome or whether I have re-created it over the years.

Either way, it was that kiss that turned Zeb and me into a different thing. Of course it wasn't the kiss itself; it was what had led up to the kiss. But after he kissed me that evening, I knew I had passed through a tunnel in my life. I had climbed into the small end of the tunnel and come out of the big end. I felt accepted and connected in a whole new way. I was in love for sure. You know how people say something melted them? Well, Zeb's kiss was so warm and soft and damp that it unhooked, unplugged, unhinged, unblocked every part of me. It left me like a gooey puddle of warm chocolate sauce when he pulled his lips away. He said he wanted to touch me? I was ready to be touched.

But he leaned back against the door and said, "Thank you." Then after a few minutes of silence, he on his side and me on mine, he started the car.

By the time he slowed down in the usual spot around the corner from the house, I had gathered myself together.

I said, "I want you to drop me off in front of the house."

"But your mother will freak. And what about Martin and Luke?"

"They'll get used to it."

"Are you sure?"

"Yeah, I'm sure."

I wasn't sure, and I didn't feel any more bold or confident than usual. It wasn't like I was thinking, I'm going to finally bring Zeb out of hiding. It was more like, at that moment, I couldn't think of one reason to keep him a secret.

He was still thinking there were lots of reasons to keep us a secret. "Are you sure?" he asked again as he pulled around the corner in full view of the house.

I laughed.

Zeb's eyes flicked back and forth between me and the house as if he expected to see someone appear with a gun.

"I better go," he said, thinking he still could sneak off without being seen. "You'll get in trouble."

"Zeb," I insisted, "I'll take care of my trouble. I want them to meet you."

"You don't get it, Josie," he protested. "People around here think I'm no good. And your mom – she won't think I'm good enough for a white girl."

His usual cool confidence had completely disappeared. He looked terrified.

"Come on in," I said. "I'll deal with her."

"Josie." He breathed a long sigh and looked deadly serious. "Are you sure you are ready for this?"

"No," I laughed. "Are you sure you are ready for this?"

"No," he said. His face relaxed, even smiled a bit.

I grabbed his hand and said, "I'm not ready. You're not ready. Can you imagine how not ready they're going to be?"

He laughed – probably not because he thought what I said was funny. Likely he laughed because something had to break the tension he was feeling and give him a boost of courage. And it worked, like one, two, three, *go*. We burst out of the car and slammed the doors. I met him at the front stairs.

"Don't worry. No one in this house bites." I giggled. "At least I don't think so." I tugged on his arm, feeling the weight of his totally resistant body. "Come on."

It was almost dark – at least 8:30, maybe 9. The living room was empty, TV was off. We met Martin coming down the hall.

"Hey," he said. "I didn't hear you. Too busy cleaning up."

"Martin," I said, "I want you to meet Zeb."

He leaned back on his heels and wiped his hands on his jeans. Almost immediately the surprise on his face was replaced by a wide smile. He threw out his hand and grabbed Zeb's hand.

"Good to meet you, son."

He pulled Zeb toward him and slapped him on the back the way men do when they meet each other.

"Yeah, nice to meet you. . . sir," Zeb mumbled.

"Martin," Martin corrected. "Call me Martin."

A knot grabbed on to my tonsils when I saw Mom come out of Luke's room down the hall. The hey-I-can't-see-any-reason-why-not attitude I had been feeling vanished when I looked at her, and suddenly my surprise introduction didn't seem such a good idea after all. At least if I had given her time to prepare, she might have dressed up or something. Instead, there she was looking more like Mom than I could have imagined. She was dressed in pink sweatpants, a loose T-shirt and no bra (not a pretty sight), and sock feet – green socks. Mom had to be the only person in the world who would wear green socks with pink sweatpants. Her hair was tied in pigtails over her ears, like a kid from the sixties.

Then it was my turn for a surprise. The instant she laid eyes on Zeb, Mom went into a flurry of grooming activity. She tugged the elastics out of her pigtails and frantically combed her fingers through her hair; she smoothed her T-shirt (which didn't help) and pulled at the legs of her sweatpants the way people do when they are trying to make the best of something that really is hopeless. All the while she was looking Zeb over up and down, and being a woman with absolutely no sense of cool she made it in-your-face obvious what she thought. After a few long seconds of silence, Mom wiped her hands on her sweatpants, stepped forward, and with a voice that sounded like a six-year-old's she said, "Aren't you going to introduce us, Jo Jo?"

"Yeah," I said, not sure how to introduce a boy, well, really a man to my mother, especially after she had just made such an ass of herself. At last I said, "Mom, this is Zeb Prince. Zeb, this is my mom, Lenore."

Zeb reached with both hands and cupped Mom's hand between his. He looked her in the eye and flashed an enormous smile.

"Wow, Lenore," he said. "I'm very happy to meet you."

"Yes," said Mom. "Me too." Then she giggled, finally self-conscious. God, what is a girl supposed to do with a mom like her?

Martin could see that I was embarrassed, so he diverted Zeb's attention. "Son," he said, "how about some tea in the kitchen?"

I followed them and Mom trailed behind me. Just as

Martin was setting cups on the table, Luke burst into the room.

"Hey, Zeb," he said simply. He looked my way. "I was wondering when you were going to bring him around."

"What do you mean?" I said.

"I mean I heard you guys were seeing each other a long time ago," he said.

"Are you telling on me?"

He laughed and reached across the table to shake Zeb's hand. "No, I'm just keeping you honest."

Chapter 15

It was pretty heavy stuff, living on the reserve. It wasn't like moving down the street or to another city. It was like moving to a different country yet still being in Canada. And I didn't choose to be there – I hadn't planned on it or got ready for it or thought it out before I got there. I just happened to get dumped there, and stayed. Pretty weird and confusing when you're fifteen. When I looked around I had a lot of thoughts, like when Rose took me on my first tour. I was thinking, Why do they live like this? And after seeing Ermaline's room and hearing Zeb's story about his parents, I wondered how it could get that bad. Even now, it's not like I have any answers. But it's pretty easy to understand why we aren't all the same.

Zeb says there are a lot of reasons the reserve is so different from other places. He says reserves don't have the same rules or government as other places in Canada – never have and still don't. Reserves and Indians have been pretty much totally shut out of the rest of the country. He also says that was then and this is now. There are a lot of people, him included, who are working to change things.

So you go around judging stuff and getting weirded out until you realize you don't know anything and you should just suck it back and watch and listen until you learn a little. It's the same anywhere. Like when you meet a grumpy-looking person on the street and you think, Why don't they just smile? And then you find out their mom just died or they got some bad news.

Enough philosophy and history. I have to finish this story and get on with my Communications assignment. A lot of things happened during my first year on the reserve. The things I'm writing might not be the most important, but they are the things I remember. And one thing I can't forget is the poem I wrote for Mrs. Hanson's English class.

A few nights later, sleep didn't come easy. It wasn't my dreams or even the constant replay of Zeb's hands and lips and eyes that kept me awake. It was my homework, which I had ignored throughout the holiday. There was one more day of spring break and I hadn't even started the English assignment that was due in less than thirty-six hours.

Mrs. Hanson assigned a poem to be written over spring break and handed in Monday morning after the holiday. It's not that I hated writing; I loved it, short stories mostly, but with everything else going on in my life I had completely forgotten about the homework.

I tossed and turned in bed, thinking about Zeb, but totally bugged about the assignment. I knew I wasn't going to be going to sleep any time soon, so I turned on the light, threw a sweatshirt over my nightie, set up pillows, a pen, paper, and a book for stability, and began to write.

Black braids, brown boy, blown away. . . I thought about the last week or so of my life. It was a love story: *Once upon a time I met a Prince*. Very funny. *Once upon a time there was a girl named Cinderella and she really did live happily ever after*. Even funnier. I doodled flowers, stars, curlicues, exclamation marks, hearts – *Josie loves Zeb*. I loved the way

Zeb Prince looked next to my name. But nothing that sounded like a poem came to mind.

Pretty soon my eyelids started to droop. I slumped lower in the pillows and set the paper up on my belly. I tried again. *I want to touch you brown boy, white girl.* I was sure I would write a love poem. What else? But the words waiting to be written weren't about a white girl or a brown boy. Suddenly my pen started moving itself. After a few minutes the page was covered with such a scrawl I could barely decipher the words. I scanned the poem and slowly began to read it out loud.

The world
Like a rocket
Took off without me
And left me. . . here. . . alone
Running. . . on broken glass
In my heart
Crouching. . . in corners and dark holes
In my brain
Cringing. . . at secret places
In my body
I'm dressing up
I've got my shoes on and my coat on and my hat on
And I'm going out
Out of here, out of there, out of nowhere
Don't print my name
Or put my picture in your magazine
Don't talk about me when you're at the kitchen table
When you are lonely
Don't come looking for me
I'm okay

You'll be okay
And someday we'll go out
Together

It wasn't my poem. Maybe it was Ermaline's – the words that were piled on top of each other on the wall. I thought about her picture and imagined her feet in pink slippers walking down the hall. I could see her brushing her teeth in the bathroom, eating mush with Martin in the morning, and sleeping in my bedroom when she was a little girl. But Ermaline was gone. The blue light was gone. I hadn't seen the *No Trespassing* sign again, and sounds no longer came from the basement. We had burned her things. The women had cleansed the room and done the cedar ceremony. Martin had painted over the printing on the wall even before Mom and Luke had a chance to read it. And now no one mentioned her name. It was as if the family had washed and folded Ermaline and put her away on the top shelf of a closet. They had shut the door on her, this time for good. But no matter how hard everyone tried to forget about her, she was still on my mind.

I tucked the paper into my English binder.

In the morning I woke up knowing exactly what I was going to do. I dressed, ate, and went out to the backyard. I picked a bouquet of daffodils and shooting stars and left them on the porch. I went back in the house looking for Luke.

"Want to give me a ride to the nursing home?" I asked when I found him eating breakfast.

He raised his head with a startled look. "Are you okay?"

"Yeah," I said. "I want to bring flowers to Grandma."

"Sure, I guess so," Luke said. "If the old Chevy's got some gas."

He stopped at the front entrance to the home.

"I'll come and visit later," he said when I got out of the car. "I have a few things to do in town."

"Thanks."

I got a vase at the nurse's station, filled it with water, and carried the flowers into Grandma's room. She was hunched over in her wheelchair, facing the garden. I watched for a few moments and then was suddenly unsure of why I was there.

"Grandma," I said.

Slowly she wheeled her chair around until it was facing the door. She had a tired look on her face.

"Did I surprise you?" I said.

"Oh, I'm not one for surprises, dear." Her face looked drawn, as if she was more bored than tired. When you're eighty-eight there's probably not much left in the world to surprise you. The look on Grandma's face said she had lived so long she could pretty much see anything coming long before it arrived.

"Beautiful," she said when she saw the flowers. "I love spring flowers." She took them from me and buried her nose in them. "What brings you to visit the old woman today, Josie?" she asked.

The truth was I still didn't know exactly why I was there. I hadn't thought, The poem is for Grandma and I have to go see her. But the moment I woke up I knew that I had to pick daffodils and head to the home. And I knew I had to bring the poem with me as well.

"Two reasons," I said. "I, well, I just wanted to visit you." Then I blurted out, "Did you know we almost have the room ready for you to move in?" Immediately I knew I shouldn't have told her. "Oh, sorry," I said. "I don't think I was supposed to say that yet."

The news lit up her face. Then her voice took a serious tone and she said, "Are you sure? Where's Luke going to go?"

"Downstairs," I said.

"Oh," she sighed, looking almost disappointed. "We'll see."

After a few moments she looked up and said, "Thank you, Josie. Now tell me what you have in that book you're holding so tightly."

"I guess that's the other reason I came here today," I said. "I wrote a poem and I want to read it to you."

"I'd love you to read me your poem," she said.

I opened the binder and pulled out the paper. "It's not really my poem," I said. "I think it belongs to. . . "

"You read your poem, Josie," she interrupted. "I will listen."

"My English teacher gave the class an assignment. We were supposed to write a poem and hand it in tomorrow."

Grandma rolled her chair up to my knee. She wove her fingers together on her lap and put her feet on the footrests of her chair. She fixed her eyes on the paper.

"The world like a rocket," I began to read. When I ended, "Together," the poem hung for a few seconds like a cloud suspended in the air. Grandma sat perfectly still, looking like someone who had just heard some tragic news.

Suddenly I thought what a stupid idea it was to read her my poem. I wanted to know more about Ermaline and I wanted Grandma to tell me, but I didn't think about how she was going to feel. Then I was scared. I wondered if bringing all this up made her sick. After a minute or so, Grandma held out her open hand and I passed her the paper. She folded it neatly into quarters, pulled out the neck of her dress, and stuffed it into her bra.

As she wiped the sleeve of her sweater across her face, the tragic look vanished and she said, "So they have cleaned out the basement."

"Yeah."

"And you helped?"

"Yeah."

"Then maybe they are ready for me to come home."

Grandma nodded her head again and again as if she was answering silent questions in her head.

"Can you come back tomorrow?" she asked. "With Martin and Lenore and Luke?"

She wheeled her chair in a semicircle over to the window, turned her side toward me, and laid her hands over her chest where the paper was stored. "I'll keep the poem until then," she said.

Now what about the English assignment deadline? Grandma dropped her chin on her chest and closed her eyes, and I sat on the bed devising excuses for Mrs. Hanson and ways to avoid bringing Martin and especially Mom to the home. I had the feeling I had really stepped out of line. What if Martin didn't want Grandma to know what Ermaline had written? Why else would he have painted the room so quickly? And why had no one said a word about her? Martin wanted her buried, for good, and now I was opening up old wounds, and bringing Grandma in on it too. You know what they say about not starting something you can't finish? Yeah, well, I had a big case of it going on.

"Hello," Luke said when he finally got back. "Sorry I took so long." He kissed Grandma on the cheek.

Without saying hello, Grandma wheeled around and patted her chest.

"I have something I want you to hear, Luke," she said.

"Speak up, Grandma." He jumped off the bed and threw his arms around her.

"Not in such a hurry," she said. "Tomorrow. I want you to bring your father and Lenore to see me. I'll talk to you all at once."

Luke threw his head back as if he was mentally tabulating his schedule for the next day. "You got it, Grandma. I'll be back. With the old man and Lenore."

"And don't you forget." She turned to me. "You're coming too."

I loved Grandma, but I wasn't used to being told what to do the way she did. I had the urge to argue. I wanted to say, I'll be here if I'm not busy. Or, What if your plan is messing me up? Or, I need my poem now, not tomorrow. But Grandma was in charge, I knew it, everyone knew it, and that left me with nothing to say. And anyway, I had started it. What *could* I say?

"Yeah," I said as we left the room. "I'll be here tomorrow after school."

I knew dealing with Mrs. Hanson was going to be easy compared to reading that poem to the whole family. That's what Grandma had up her sleeve and I wasn't looking forward to it one bit.

"What's she up to?" Luke asked as I raced down the corridor behind him.

It was too complicated to tell him about the poem, and I knew he hadn't even seen Ermaline's room, so I said, "I don't know."

Driving home Luke asked, "That Zeb okay to you?"

"Yeah," I said.

"Really? Is he good to you?"

"Yeah, really. He's a nice guy."

He tapped his finger on the steering wheel and hummed along with the radio.

"Don't you like him?" I asked.

"No, no, it's not that." Luke looked sideways and squinted his eyes as if he was trying to see inside my brain. "He's got a pretty bad rep. He's been into some pretty brutal shit, man. I just wanted you to be okay."

"I'm okay," I said.

I was better than okay. Zeb was awesome, Luke was great, and Martin was pretty good if you had to have a stepfather. I had gone from zero to three men in my life, and they were all good ones.

Chapter 16

Martin said, "When should I tell Grandma we can bring her home?"

He looked at Mom while she stared straight ahead and narrowed her eyes, as if this was the first time she had thought about the question.

"Why wait?" she said.

Why wait? Can you imagine? Mom said it as if she hadn't been the one who had dug her heels into the ground for so long that she was buried up to her knees. As if Martin was the one holding things up. "I think we should get her home as soon as possible," Mom said. "How about Sunday?"

She nodded in agreement with herself. "Yeah, Sunday would be a good day. We could pick her up around noon. We'll have her all settled in by supper."

If I was Martin I would have sworn at Mom or strangled her, but he reached across the car seat and squeezed her shoulder.

"Yeah, Sunday is a good day," he said.

We looked like a family of ducklings trailing behind Mom through the corridors. She was charging toward Grandma's room like she had the day under control. She thought we were visiting so she could tell Grandma when to move home. Mom didn't have a clue what Grandma had in store for her that evening. No one else did either, although I had an inkling of what was going to happen.

When we arrived, Grandma was sitting in her wheelchair in a semicircle of chairs by the bed. Mom barged right in, pushed the chairs aside, and threw her arms around Grandma as if they were old friends.

"Good to see you, Grandma," she said. She pulled another chair out of the way to give Martin and Luke room to hug Grandma.

Grandma ignored Mom and motioned to me to sit on the bed.

"Here," she said, tugging on the chairs to re-form the semicircle. "You sit there." She beckoned to Luke and Mom to sit on the far chairs and then pointed to Martin and nodded at the chair beside her wheelchair.

"I want you all close to the bed so you can hear."

The confident smile on Mom's face was slowly replaced by a look of confusion. Grandma's take-charge directions had whisked Mom's determination away like a stiff wind. She slouched in the chair and looked at Martin as if to say, Tell her about Sunday. Martin smiled at Mom and watched Grandma. The time to tell her about Sunday would come.

Grandma reached her hand down the front of her dress and pulled out the poem. Why did I let her get me into this? I took the paper out of her hand, unfolded it, and slumped forward self-consciously. From under my eyelids I scanned the room. All eyes were directed my way. Luke's face was amused and confused. He was along for the ride. He leaned back in his chair with his arm stretched around Mom's shoulder and his ankle hooked to his knee. Mom was pouting. Her moment had been spoiled and she looked at me as if I was responsible. Martin leaned against Grandma's wheelchair, his eyes fixed on the paper and a look of patient anticipation on his face. The arrangement looked like something straight out of a weird movie. Grandma was the director. It was her show; she was bright and chipper and in control, just the way she liked it. We were the actors playing our roles, speaking our lines, and for a moment the spotlights were on me.

She flicked her finger toward me and nodded her head as if to say, Start reading. I felt like someone had ripped off my clothes and stuffed my mouth full of dry soda crackers. Grandma flicked her finger again and said, "Read."

I looked at Luke and then looked at the first words, *The world*. "I, uh." I paused and looked Grandma's way with panic. I wanted her to rescue me. I couldn't start reading. People don't just sit in a circle in a room and read each other stupid poems.

Grandma said, "I want Josie to read you a poem. She brought it to me yesterday and I want you all to hear it."

Her short introduction was better than nothing. And there I was, no way out and not much I could do about it. Given the situation I had no choice but to read the poem, no matter how ridiculous I felt.

I cleared my throat. "I wrote this poem for school. It was due today but Mrs. Hanson said I could bring it in tomorrow." I was saying anything to avoid beginning. "It sort of wrote itself."

I stared at the paper and froze. I felt hot and prickly, like someone was asking me to show my private parts – the bits right inside that I never even show myself.

The world.

The room was dead quiet as I read. I kept my eyes on the paper, but I could see, or maybe I could feel, that they were listening so closely they were barely breathing. When I read the last words I peered over the paper at Grandma and Martin. Their heads leaned towards each other, eyes fixed on the paper and hands clutching the armrest of the wheelchair. I folded the paper and stuffed it into my purse. That's it. I dragged my butt off the bed, stood up, and I would have shot out of the room if I wasn't trapped in the circle.

Luke broke the silence and said, "Holy crap, that's a good poem. Where the hell you get that from?"

Grandma ignored Luke and motioned for me to sit back on the bed.

She said, "Now I'm going to tell you all something I should have told you a long time ago."

She told us the story of her life. Her mother died when she was a teenager and, soon after, her father left them. She was the oldest of ten kids so she raised her brothers and sisters. They were poor, dead poor. They ate potatoes and onions a farmer dropped off for them, and the men in the community brought them fish. She cooked fish-head soup and fish stew and for Christmas dinner she boiled smoked fish. Things got better when she got married. Her husband helped build the house and she had Arnie and Martin. Then, only a couple of months after Ermaline was born, her husband died. A few years later Grandma got sick with tuberculosis.

"I fought the TB," Grandma said, looking through the window as if she was looking into a mirror to the past. "I got to stay home with my baby girl until she was six years old. Then they came and took me to the hospital. Oh, walking down that road away from the house. . . " Grandma stopped, took a heavy breath, and continued. "Martin was there, standing at the door. I don't know where Arnie was. I never knew where Arnie was. Martin promised he would look after little Ermaline. I remember him shouting, 'Don't worry, Mom. We'll be fine.' Ermaline sat on his shoulders and waved goodbye."

Grandma said she was in and out of the hospital for the next eleven years.

"The TB got so bad they wouldn't let me out. If I did convince them to spring me loose, I could only go home for a day or two, and it got so that I hardly knew Ermaline. Martin raised Ermaline just like I had raised my brothers and sisters. I was proud of him. He sent me Ermaline's report cards and pictures from school. She was so pretty and smart. Her teachers said she should go to university and become a teacher."

Grandma's eyes were dry but her chest heaved like she was crying, only on the inside.

"Then I got the phone call from Martin," Grandma said. "And they let me out of the hospital only long enough to attend her funeral. That was the last time I saw my little girl. And no one has said a word about her since."

I had never seen Luke looking so surprised. In fact, I can say he looked totally shocked. Then his face got serious and he said, "Why didn't you tell me? I didn't know what was in that room until Anne and Cecelia came to clean it out. Up until that day I thought Ermaline died in an accident." He paused for a second and added, "I knew there was something strange down there. The room was always locked and Dad said it was full of junk and out of bounds."

He settled back into his chair, folded his arms, and shook his head. Then he shot a look at me. "That blue light?" he said.

I shrugged.

Mom was completely dumbfounded. She looked like she

was watching the weirdest afternoon talk show she had ever seen. Only it was real. Frozen and half leaning against Luke, her lips looked parched, her mouth open slightly. I could hear air whistling through her teeth. Suddenly her eyes popped wide open as if someone had just turned the lights on at the end of a movie.

"Oh," she said right out of the blue, "did Martin tell you? We have a room ready for you. We're going to move you home on Sunday."

Grandma turned her wheelchair toward Mom. "Wonderful, Lenore," she said. "Maybe this story has a happy ending."

Yeah, I thought, and there's really a Santa Claus and Cinderella.

Chapter 17

It's not done till it's done. You've heard that before. It's true. And we weren't ready till we were ready. It took almost a year to prepare for Grandma to come home. And I don't mean just cleaning out the basement room. It was about timing again. There were things standing in the way that we couldn't acknowledge, like an elephant in the room that no one wanted to talk about and no one could see around. Martin had started the process when he opened the door and cleaned out the room, but after the women left it was like he buried the subject again. He painted the walls before Mom or Luke got to read them. He shut the door again and reburied the subject. It was Grandma who finally walked the elephant out of the room. And then the way was finally clear.

The phone rang.

"Josie, honey," Grandma said. "Could you get Martin to the phone?"

It was Sunday morning. Mom was up and eating breakfast with Martin and me. She was ready, as she had said, to move Grandma home.

"It's for you," I said to Martin. "It's Grandma."

Martin took the phone.

"Uh-huh." He nodded. "Sure." He looked confused. "Well,

if that's what the doctor says." There was a long pause. Mom lifted her head, waiting for what Martin was about to say. "So you won't be coming home until Friday?"

Mom set her spoon down with a deliberate motion and threw her hands up in a huff as if to say, What next? Like she had put in some giant effort to prepare for Grandma to get out of the hospital. And now her plans were ruined.

"No, no," said Martin. "That's fine. Whatever's best for you."

Mom snapped her tongue behind her teeth and then spat through her lips, "What do you mean, whatever is best for *you?*"

Martin stared at the phone to avoid Mom's side talk.

"Martin," she said. When he continued to ignore her she clapped her hands. "Martin! We had it all planned for today. Now what?"

Now what? Grandma waits six months for Mom to get it together so she can move home, and then when Grandma delays the plans for less than one week, Mom has a hissy fit? A woman who never has anything to do from one day to the next anyway? I used to think I could read Mom like a book, but that was when our life consisted of Mom and me and no interruptions. Moving to Martin's place had complicated Mom's life, putting her back up against the wall more than once, so I wasn't always sure which way she would move. I don't think she knew either.

"Martin," she said, "what about what's best for *us?* We had today all planned."

"Okay, Mom," Martin said without giving Mom a glance. "Sure. We'll be around to visit this afternoon anyway."

"Martin," Mom said when he hung up the phone. Her voice was reaching a critical pitch. She sat straight-backed and bug-eyed in her chair, and if you had stuck a pin in her she would have exploded.

Martin turned around and stood an arm's length away from Mom. He breathed in a long breath that seemed to expand his body so it was bigger than usual and looked her square on. "Lenore," said Martin, "Mom has tests at the hospital tomorrow and Wednesday. She'll wait for results and be home Friday."

"She could have had tests done last week, the week before," Mom said. "Why did she wait until this week? She knew we had it all planned."

There was a pause in the conversation. One of Martin's famous silences, designed to make Mom listen to herself. Good luck. But I had time to think that Grandma had arranged her tests deliberately to foil Mom's good intentions. I mentally shook my head. Grandma wasn't the kind of woman to be pushed around. She might have been eighty-eight and stuck in a wheelchair, but she was in control of herself and intended to stay that way. She wasn't about to give that up to Mom.

Mom hadn't thought it out, I was sure. But I could tell that she felt Grandma's challenge as plain as two boys calling each other out in the schoolyard. She felt it from the bottom of her gut.

"She's stubborn, your mom," Mom said. "She just wants to get her own way. That's what this is about."

It wasn't Martin's turn yet. He waited.

"We had it all planned, Martin." Mom slouched down in her chair a little. Her voice had lost its high pitch. "Now what about supper? We were going to have a family supper."

Martin didn't move.

Mom slurped her coffee.

"I'm going to visit her," Martin said. "Are you coming?"

"I guess so," said Mom.

That was the thing about Mom. She could feel a challenge, but she didn't know how to follow it up. She might still feel angry and confronted, but she couldn't hold on to her point. Now, with the wind taken out of her sails, she was giving up. But Martin and I both knew it wasn't over between Mom and Grandma.

Friday after school I flew up the front stairs, burst into the living room, and stopped, stunned. Oprah was interviewing a mother of eight boys (can you imagine?), Mom was sitting in her usual place, a haze of blue smoke lingering above her head, and Martin was whittling cedar at his table. Nothing strange about that scene except that Grandma sat on the chair next to Mom as if she had been there every day for the last century.

After waiting forever for Grandma to come home, all of a sudden it's no fuss, no muss, no fanfare and she's sitting in the living room as if she had never left.

"Come over here, honey," she said. She pointed to a chair and beckoned me to pull it close to her. "What did you do at school today?"

She held my hands while I thought of something. How do you answer a question like that? I wasn't used to anyone asking me about school.

"And where is that young Jackson girl?" she asked.

"You mean Rose?" I said.

"She's your friend, isn't she?"

"Yeah. She's coming over."

The conversation carried on, Grandma and I talking

about school and friends. Mom glanced over. At first I thought she was miffed that we were interrupting Oprah, and then I think she was pleased.

When Rose arrived, Grandma shifted into her wheelchair. "You girls follow me," she said. "I have something I want to show you in my room."

She didn't show us anything; she told us something. June 21 was Mom and Martin's first anniversary and Grandma was going to throw a party. An open invitation, she said, to the family and anyone else who wanted to attend.

"And I want you girls to invite your friends," said Grandma. "I want everyone to come. And I want it to be a surprise."

June 21 was a fabulously sunny day. Grandma took Mom and Martin out for lunch while Zeb, Luke, Rose and I, Rose's mother, and some other women from the reserve decorated the house with balloons and a banner that said *Congratulations Martin and Lenore*. We cooked and arranged food on platters.

When Mom and Martin got home, the house was full of people. People I had seen on the street, Rose's neighbours, Martin's cousins and friends, kids, adults, teenagers I had seen on the bus, people I had never seen before. The big guy and the guy with the Coke-bottle glasses from school were there, and Rose had invited Shelley.

"Surprise!" everyone shouted when Mom and Martin appeared in the living room.

Grandma smiled. Martin tried to give an I-knew-this-was-planned look, but he was surprised, no doubt about it. Mom didn't try to hide anything. Her mouth dropped open in a state of shock and semi-panic. Martin pulled her over to the banner, put his arms around her, and planted a big kiss on her mouth.

It was as if an uneven wind had blown through the room. Some people whistled and clapped, others stared as if they were watching a restricted movie and Mom and Martin had just done the thing that made it restricted. Martin grinned and Mom was dumbstruck. I moved close to Zeb, who had a quizzical look on his face, as if he didn't know what to feel. It was Mom and Martin's coming-out party, the grand announcement: Hey, everyone, look this way, here's Martin's new wife. Up until that moment their relationship had been tucked away in the closet. Now it was hanging out for everyone to see.

Grandma wheeled to the front of the crowd and cleared her throat. A hush fell over the room. She cocked her finger at Luke, who came up and stood by her side. He leaned over as she spoke in his ear.

When he straightened up he said, "Grandma is thankful you all came to the house today. She called you all here to celebrate Dad and Lenore's anniversary."

Grandma tugged on Luke's sleeve. He bent down and she whispered in his ear again.

Luke nodded and said, "Grandma says that she is happy Martin is married, and she wants to welcome Lenore into the Angus family."

Grandma clapped her hands and nodded her head. Slowly all the people in the room did the same thing. A few people shouted, "Way to go, Martin," and "Hurray," but mostly the crowd was quiet.

After a long pause Grandma pulled Luke close and spoke in his ear.

"And Grandma says that it is a good thing that Lenore has brought Josie, her beautiful blonde daughter, to live with us." Luke smirked at me. The beautiful blonde part obviously came from Grandma. Luke was only doing his job.

Grandma lifted both her hands with her palms up. She looked at me with a huge smile and said, "Thank you, Josie. Thank you. You are welcome in our home." Then she looked around the room, still holding her arms up, and said, "Thank you, everyone. Thank you."

It was the last day of something and the first day of something else. I wasn't quite sure what had happened, but it felt like Grandma had cleared the air and opened the way for Mom and me to be part of the family and the reserve. I was overwhelmed by a sense of relief. I didn't need to apologize. I was supposed to be there.

"Are you Josie?" a little boy asked.

"Do you see any other beautiful blonde girl around?" Zeb said.

The kid scrunched up his nose.

Zeb and I were heading outside with Rose and a plate of watermelon when Arnie came up the stairs.

"Congratulations?" he shouted when he read the banner.

People shifted uneasily. A few said, "Hey, Arnie," and "How's it going?" Most of the people ignored him. He didn't look like he'd been drinking, but he was in some kind of mood that I wanted to avoid.

"Hey, Blondie," he said. "Aren't you going to offer me some watermelon?"

"Here." Zeb took a piece and handed it to him.

Arnie grabbed the fruit.

"Blondie," he blurted out. "Get over here. I want to talk to you."

He was about to lunge toward me when Mom walked out of the kitchen and directly between us. Bad timing for her. The room was hot and quiet. Anticipation hung in the room like smoke – what was Arnie going to do? If he had been drunk we could have laughed him off, but there was an ominous threat in his voice, and I wanted to get out of there.

"Oh," he said belligerently. "Lenore. Baby. I'll talk to you instead."

Mom, completely unprepared, said, "Arnie?"

"Yeah, Arnie," he said. "You know me. Your brother-in-law."

He leaned toward Mom. Zeb moved closer, ready to intervene.

"Yeah, Lenore, baby, I'm just the old rubby-dub brother-in-law." Arnie's eyes were fierce. He had a thick pungent body odour around him that wasn't mixed with alcohol. "And surprise, surprise, lady. I'm sober."

Mom's knees were shaking, and although her mouth was open, no words were coming out.

"What the fuck are you white people doing coming and living on the reserve?" Arnie shouted as clearly as if he hadn't had a drink for months. "That's what I want to know. What the fuck are you and your little daughter doing living in my house?"

Mom almost collapsed. What had started out to be a great day was quickly turning into a nightmare. Face-to-face confrontation with Arnie was more than Mom could handle.

"You fucking white people think you own everything. Like you can go anywhere you please." Arnie was on a roll and nothing was going to stop him.

Except me. It felt like someone had pulled a trigger in

my brain – I snapped. Arnie wasn't going to spoil my day or embarrass my mom. If no one else was going to stop him, I was.

"Take your watermelon and go outside," I said.

"You say something, little girl?" Arnie growled.

"I said go outside, Arnie." I stared him square in his face. He towered over me, beginning to look confused. "And you know what else? You want to know why these fucking white people are living on the reserve? You want to know, Arnie? 'Cause I want to tell you."

He recoiled against the wall as I moved closer to him.

"We live here because Mom fell in love with Martin," I shouted. I hadn't spoken so loudly since I hollered at Mom when she announced she was getting married. "Yeah, for your information we are here because Mom loves your brother. Is there some law against that? And your brother loves my mom. He married her. No one handcuffed him and made him do it."

Arnie was speechless. So it was still my turn and I was going to take it.

"And I'm here because she's my mom. You got a problem with that? Arnie?" I punched my words out like a prizefighter. "Do you?"

He couldn't say anything and I couldn't shut up.

"It's not like we came down the road and said, Hey, this looks like a nice place, let's move in."

By this time Arnie had a half grin on his face.

"Okay, little girl," he said. "Okay."

Mom staggered to the sofa and fell into her corner in front of the TV. Arnie struck his hand out to Zeb and said, "Arnie, the asshole brother-in-law."

Zeb said, "Zeb, the boyfriend."

Rose said, "Way to go, Josie."

Gradually conversations started up again in the room. Rose, Zeb, and I headed outside with the watermelon and Arnie followed us. For the rest of the evening he seemed to enjoy himself. He talked to people without being obnoxious, and I didn't see any paper bags or bottles under his arm. And this time Luke didn't need to drag him off to the bedroom.

It was a little after ten when everyone finally left. Rose and Zeb helped clean up before he drove her home. I lay in my bed and listened to Mom and Martin talking in their room, Luke's music filtering through the floor vents, and the tattered old warrior flag fluttering in the breeze. I looked at the chipped and peeled paint on the ceiling and thought about Ermaline and Grandma. I could almost hear kids running around the house and see Grandma chasing after them. When I closed my eyes I heard stories I had never heard before and I knew this was only a beginning.

Epilogue

So here it is. I'm finally finished. Now I can get down to writing 500 words on why I like to draw. On perspective – the part I like best about drawing. I think I've cleared up the question about where I'm from, at least for now. I have a better understanding about where I sit and the angle I see things from. I can't wait to hear what Rose and Zeb think of this story. They'll each have a different perspective, that's for sure.

I'll print it and give Grandma a copy. Her eyesight's not too good anymore, but Martin said he would read the story to her. And Mom? I doubt she'll get through it. She doesn't read too much, never did. I'm sure it comes as no surprise that Mom hasn't changed much. TV, cigarettes, but her and Martin seem to be hanging in there.

Luke's got a job in town and a live-in girlfriend, Angel. And I hear they have a baby coming.

Oh, I forgot to mention. I called Katy and Sarah the other day. They're working at the mall. I'm going to get together with them the next time I go home. I'll give them a copy of this story. I'm sure they'll have another perspective altogether.

Acknowledgements:

Thanks to Diane Morriss at Sono Nis Press for her unwaivering support, advice and creative eye. Thanks to a wonderful team of editors—Laura Peetoom, Audrey McClellan, Margaret Tessman, and Chris Nichol. Once again thanks to Julia Bell for her beautiful art. And thanks to all the other white girls who have exchanged stories with me over the years.

Sylvia Olsen was born and brought up in Victoria, British Columbia. A blonde, blue-eyed Canadian girl of English and German descent, Sylvia married into the Tsartlip First Nation when she was seventeen. It was only three years after her marriage that Sylvia realized that Canadian law made her a Status Indian. She has lived and worked and raised her four children in the Tsartlip community now for over thirty years.

Being a white girl on the reserve was one of the formative experiences of Sylvia's life. Living on the reserve has given Sylvia an intimate and sustained view of the world of First Nations/non-First Nations relations in Canada. And like Josie in *White Girl*, the reserve provided a mirror in which Sylvia faced "whiteness" at a very early age and in a way that shaped the rest of her life.

Always curious and lacking ready answers to her questions about why people treat each other the way they do, she returned to school at age 35. Sylvia received her Masters in History, specializing in Native/white relations in Canada. As a writer, she often finds herself exploring the in-between place where First Nations and non-First Nations people meet. Sylvia currently works in the area of First Nations community management, with a focus on on-reserve housing.

Also by Sylvia Olsen:

The Girl With a Baby

1-55039-142-9

- BC Bestseller
- Winner of an Our Choice Award and nominated for the Saskatchewan Young Readers' Choice Snow Willow Award and The Stellar Award: the new Teen Readers' Choice Award of BC.

The perfect daughter in a less-than-perfect family, Jane Williams now has a daughter of her own. … This is a right-of-passage story, joining the strength and tradition of Jane's [Native] heritage as given to her by her people with her personal struggle to face and win her own battles. This contemporary novel beautifully blends a realistic story of teenage life with a unique view of an old and largely unknown Native culture. This is a common story told uncommonly well."

– Starred review, *School Library Journal*

No Time to Say Goodbye

Children's Stories of Kuper Island Residential School

1-55039-121-6

- Adopted by the B.C. Teachers' Federation
- Saskatchewan Young Readers' Snow Willow Award Nominee

No Time to Say Goodbye is a fictional account of five children sent to aboriginal boarding school, based on the recollections of a number of Tsartlip First Nations people. Taken by government agents from Tsartlip Day School to live at Kuper Island Residential School, the children are isolated on the small island and life becomes regimented by the strict school routine. They experience the pain of homesickness and confusion while trying to adjust to a world completely different from their own. Their lives are no longer organized by fishing, hunting and family, but by bells, line-ups and chores. In spite of the harsh realities of the residential school, the children find adventure in escape, challenge in competition, and camaraderie with their fellow students.

Critical acclaim for White Girl

Starred review - BookList

"White people were just people. It was the other people who stuck out." That is how it has always been for Canadian teen Josie, until her mom marries Martin, "a real ponytail Indian," and they move to his home on the reserve. Suddenly Josie is "Blondie," alone, and a stranger, taunted by bullies and longing for her friends back at the mall. She eventually finds a friend who shows her around the reserve, and later, a boyfriend; but it is the complex family story of her family that is the heart of the novel. Josie's mother has never been much of a parent. Martin and his mother and son, who are drawn without reverence or stereotyping, are strong and kind. But Martin has done time in jail, his older brother is a drunk, and there are terrible secrets to uncover, even in a place where it seems everyone knows everything about everybody. Olsen, a blonde, blue-eyed Canadian who married a Tsartlip Indian when she was in her teens, writes from the inside, especially about stereotypes that go both ways, and about the heartbreak on the reserve. Occasionally, the message is spelled out too clearly ("We're all different. Get over it"), but even then the talk is contemporary and relaxed, and the characters will hold readers as much as the novel's extraordinary sense of place. —*Hazel Rochman*

Starred review - School Library Journal.

Following her highly acclaimed *Girl with a Baby* (Sono Nis, 2004), Olsen scores another winner. Josie Jessop, 15, moves onto an Indian reserve when her mother marries Martin Angus, whom her mom describes as a "real ponytail Indian." Angry at losing her "normal" life and friends to become a stepdaughter and the target of racial conflict on the reserve, Josie finds untapped integrity within herself, a supportive new family complete with a grandmother, the truest friend she has ever had, and a hot love interest to boot. . . . *White Girl* is an outstanding story on many levels, and a much-needed addition to the body of contemporary Indian literature for teens.

—*Sean George*, MEMPHIS-SHELBY COUNTY PUBLIC LIBRARY & INFORMATION CENTER, MEMPHIS, TN